S0-CBQ-187

DATE DUE

AUG 02

OCT 0 7 2002		
NOV 1 8 '03 JUN 08 04		
GAYLORD		PRINTED IN U.S.A.

The Dead of Brooklyn

Also by Robert J. Randisi
in Large Print:

No Exit from Brooklyn

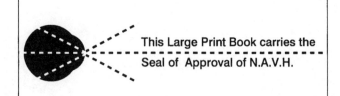

This Large Print Book carries the
Seal of Approval of N.A.V.H.

Robert J. Randisi

The Dead of Brooklyn

A Nick Delvecchio Novel

Thorndike Press • Waterville, Maine

JACKSON COUNTY LIBRARY SERVICES
MEDFORD OREGON 97501

Copyright © 1991 by Robert J. Randisi.

All rights reserved.

Published in 2002 by arrangement with
Dominick Abel Literary Agency, Inc.

Thorndike Press Large Print Mystery Series.

The tree indicium is a trademark of Thorndike Press.

The text of this Large Print edition is unabridged.
Other aspects of the book may vary from the original edition.

Cover design by Thorndike Press Staff.

Set in 16 pt. Plantin by Al Chase.

Printed in the United States on permanent paper.

Library of Congress Cataloging-in-Publication Data
Randisi, Robert J.
    The dead of Brooklyn : a Nick Delvecchio novel /
Robert J. Randisi.
        p. cm.
    ISBN 0-7862-4399-6 (lg. print : hc : alk. paper)
    1. Delvecchio, Nick (Fictitious character) — Fiction.
    2. Private investigators — New York (State) — New York
    — Fiction.   3. Brooklyn (New York, N.Y.) — Fiction.
    4. Clergy — Fiction.   5. Large type books.   I. Title.
    PS3568.A53 D4 2002
    813′.54—dc21   2002067280

To my friend Pat Lobrutto.
Thanks for sharing both your
encouragement and your courage.

1

It was what I call one of my "Brooklyn Blues" days. I was thirty-two, a bachelor, doing my own laundry in the neighborhood Laundromat. On top of that, I hadn't had a case for a couple of weeks and money was getting tight. Did I say tight? It was damn well cutting off my circulation. The last five hundred dollars I had made had not gone very far.

I have done laundry in Laundromats when being there was a bachelor's delight. In fact, up until about six months ago there were these three girls who were roommates living in the neighborhood and they used to take turns doing the laundry. In the summer those girls would come in dressed in shorts and halter tops of bathing suits, and in the winter — when they took off their coats — they'd be wearing tight jeans and leg warmers. I mean, all during that time I looked forward to my time in the Laundromat, but they only lived in the neighborhood for a few months and then moved, and laundry went back to being a chore.

As a whole, the regular people who used

this Laundromat were pretty nice, but they were no great shakes to look at. Mrs. Goldstein is a woman in her late fifties who sort of adopted me — telling me which detergent to use, and which fabric softener, and "Oy, boychick, don't wash those in cold water!" — but she kind of resembled the south end of a battleship going north; Big "Mad Dog" Bolinsky, a bruiser who worked for the Department of Sanitation, looked like the *whole* ship; Mr. Quinn, the Greek grocer, was in his late fifties also, and don't think Mrs. Goldstein didn't know he was a widower, just as she was a widow.

And then there was Sam. Her real name was Samantha Karson, but she wrote her romance novels under the name "Kit Karson" — when she sold them, that is. I think she has sold three, so far, huge tomes with lurid covers showing big breasts on the women and bare chests on the men. Sam lives across the hall from me and takes time out from her computer from time to time to take in a movie with me, or to do her laundry. She's not the neatest person in the world, but she's pretty and easy to get along with. We're very good buddies, and we've never slept together.

So it was on one of my Brooklyn Blues days, when I was feeling slightly sorry for

8

myself, when Linda Kellogg walked in.

She had never been there before and naturally became the center of attention right away — with me because of her good looks, and with Mrs. Goldstein because she's the neighborhood busybody.

Nobody spoke to her beyond saying hello because that wasn't the way things were done. If she came back again, indicating that she might become a regular, then everyone would make an effort to get to know her. I would have made an effort right off the bat, but as she took the machine right next to mine I noticed that she was wearing a wedding ring.

I noticed a few other things too. She had a bruise alongside her left eye, and as she was putting her clothes into the machine I noticed a blouse with blood on it. When she turned my way at one point, I saw that her lip was split and puffed on one side. The lip and the bruise looked to be about five or six days old. Three days ago she would have looked a lot worse. This could all have been the result of anything from a mugging to a family dispute, and I really didn't give it a second thought after leaving the Laundromat that day.

The second time she came around I found out her name — from Mrs. Goldstein, of course — and during the course of the next couple of weeks she came in every Tuesday and Friday — Friday being my regular day — and Mrs. Goldstein, who was at the Laundromat three days a week, busied herself getting all the dope. (Mrs. Goldstein was a widow who lived alone, so you know she didn't *have* to go to the Laundromat three times a week just to do her *laundry*.)

Linda usually had a small bruise here or there when she came — she *could* have just been clumsy — but finally one Friday I noticed her talking to Mrs. Goldstein and crying, and that was when nice Mrs. Goldstein dragged her over to me.

"This quiet fella is Nick Delvecchio, Linda. He's a nice enough boy to be Jewish." That was the highest praise Mrs. Goldstein could have given me. "He's also the best private detective in Brooklyn." A dubious distinction at best.

Of course, Mrs. Goldstein is addicted to mystery novels that feature private eyes. She was always trying to get Sam to write one instead of those "meshugge" romance novels. At that very moment she had a paperback copy of something called *Jackpot* by Bill Pronzini in her voluminous purse.

"Hello," Linda said meekly.

"We've met in passing," I said. I was

starting to get a picture I didn't like.

"Linda has a problem, Nick," Mrs. Goldstein said, "and I told her you could help her."

"Is that a fact? What kind of a problem?" I asked, noticing the mouse she had beneath her right eye. The first day I had laid eyes on her was one of my Brooklyn Blues days, and I had the feeling this was going to turn into one, too.

I hate domestic cases. Nobody ever wins. What was worse, I couldn't very well turn this one down with the rent coming due, and with Mrs. Goldstein looking at me the way she was. Besides, I had already turned down a case recently, for personal reasons. I couldn't afford to take any more high moral stands, not at this point.

"Tell him, dearie," Mrs. Goldstein was urging Linda Kellogg.

Linda looked from Mrs. Goldstein to me a couple of times and I said, "Mrs. Goldstein, isn't your machine finished?"

"What?" the older woman said, looking behind her. Her wash was still being swirled inside her machine, but never let it be said that Mrs. Goldstein couldn't take a hint.

"Hmm," she said, giving me the eye. "You help her, Nick. She's a nice girl."

"We'll see, Mrs. Goldstein."

11

"Hmm," she said again, and left us to go back to her machine and her book.

"She's a nice old busybody," I said.

"I like her."

"Do you want to tell me about it, or do you want to let her think you're telling me about it?"

"I think I'll talk to you, Mr. Delvecchio. Even if you can't help me, it might do me some good."

"All right," I said. "You don't mind if I fold my shirts and . . . other things while we talk, do you?"

"Oh," she said, as if the thought of a man folding his own belongings surprised her, "I'll do that."

She walked to my pile of laundry and began to talk and fold at the same time. I hoped she was using some sort of universal fold, and that I wouldn't have to refold my things so they'd fit in my drawer.

Put succinctly — which she did not do — it seemed that over the past few months, since even before they moved to this neighborhood, her husband had taken to beating her up on occasion. That was what she said, "On occasion." I asked her to define "occasion." She said that sometimes he would come home from work angry and hit her, even if she had cooked him his favorite dinner.

"Is it always after work?" I asked.

"Yes."

"But you can never predict it?"

"No," she said. "Most nights he's fine, very loving, and other nights the slightest thing will set him off. I can't understand it."

"How long have you been married?"

"Two years."

"Do you have any children?"

"No."

"Have you ever been pregnant?"

She frowned and said, "No, I said we never had any children."

That wasn't exactly what she'd said, but I let it pass. I figured there was no point in bringing up the question of miscarriages. I'd known men who beat their pregnant wives into miscarriages, but that didn't seem to apply here.

"And this is only a recent development in your marriage?"

"Yes."

"Had he ever struck you before these incidents?"

"No, never." She answered all the questions without looking at me, but looking at the laundry she was folding.

"Linda . . . do you think he might have a girlfriend?" I was fairly sure that would be what was uppermost in her mind. I was wrong. She looked at me with shock written all over her face. I couldn't believe that the thought had never occurred to her.

"I *never* thought of that."

Was she on the level? Could she really be that innocent? Or was I just too much of a cynic?

Probably a little of both.

"Linda, what about drugs?"

"No," she said firmly, "never."

I shrugged to myself. She may have been sure that he had no girlfriend and no involvement with drugs, but to me they were very real possibilities for the cause of the problem she was describing.

"Linda, what is it you would like me to do?"

"I — I would want you to find out what is making him so angry," she said, folding a pair of my boxer shorts. "You see, if he didn't come home so angry, then it wouldn't happen. He wouldn't have any reason to hit me. Do you see that?"

No, I didn't see that. I didn't believe in men hitting women for any reason. I felt that men who beat their wives shouldn't have gotten married in the first place, but then what did I know? I'd never been married, I'd never even lived with a woman.

"Have you ever thought about leaving him?"

That shocked her as much as the question about a possible girlfriend. In fact, it shocked her into looking at me.

"And go where? I have no family. I barely have any friends. I wouldn't have anyplace to go, Mr. Delvecchio. Besides, I love my husband. Will you help me? I can pay you."

I almost told her not to worry about that, but since I was so short of money, I kept my mouth shut. Maybe I would just charge her one month's rent and be done with it. I'd snoop around some, see if her husband had a girlfriend, or a nose-candy habit, see what was making him so mad. If I didn't find something out in a day or two . . . well, that would be that.

She had finished folding my laundry and was just staring at me, waiting for my answer.

Helpless before the so completely innocent look in her eyes, I said, "I'll try and find out what makes him so angry."

She put her hand on my arm and said, "Thank you, Mr. Delvecchio, thank you."

I smiled halfheartedly and said, "Call me Nick."

2

Linda Kellogg's husband's name was Dan, and he worked as a dispatcher for a trucking firm with an office in the Greenpoint section of Brooklyn. According to Linda, the position was a promotion for him, and the raise in salary was what had enabled them to move to a better neighborhood. My block of Sackett Street wasn't quite in Park Slope and was almost in south Brooklyn. The bodega on the corner had a sign in the window that said, "No selling drugs on the street in front of the store." That was because they probably sold drugs *inside* the store and didn't want the competition. If the Kelloggs considered this a better neighborhood, I hated to think where they'd been living before.

I had followed Dan Kellogg to and from work for a week, and so far I had discovered two things: I didn't know what was making him so angry, and he didn't seem to have a girlfriend — which, for all I knew, might have been what was making him so angry.

I spoke to Linda after the week was up and she told me that Dan hadn't laid a finger on her since she hired me. I asked if she thought he knew about me and she said she was sure he didn't. She asked me to please stay on the case for a little while longer and I agreed. Once again she assured me that she could pay me. I wondered where she was going to get the money, and how she would explain its disappearance to her husband without getting beaten up again.

After two weeks total there was still no indication that *anything* was bothering Dan Kellogg, and there was still no sign of a girlfriend. In fact, he hardly ever went out for lunch. Maybe the problem had resolved itself.

I felt guilty taking a fee from Linda, and when she asked me how much she owed me I charged her for one week instead of two without telling her. It was five days' work, since Kellogg didn't work on the weekends. I managed to come out of it with a month's rent, plus some grocery money. We severed our business relationship in the same place where it had started, at the Laundromat, and after Linda left, Mrs. Goldstein came over.

"Did you help her, Nicky?"

17

"I tried, Mrs. Goldstein, but I couldn't find out anything."

"No girlfriend?"

"No girlfriend."

"So," Mrs. Goldstein said, "that's something. You put her mind to rest about that."

"Yeah," I said, "that's something." I didn't bother telling her that I was the one who had put the idea into Linda's head in the first place. "I think maybe this problem may have solved itself, Mrs. Goldstein."

Looking doubtful, she said, "Mark my words, boychick. Problems very rarely solve themselves. Somebody usually has to solve them."

"I'll remember that, ma'am," I said, and left with my clean laundry. I hoped that in this particular case, she was wrong.

3

The following week I walked into the Laundromat and got from Mrs. Goldstein the dirtiest look she could muster.

"So, Mister Smart-Guy?" she asked, folding her arms across her ample chest.

"So what, Mrs. Goldstein?"

"What have you got to say for yourself?"

"About what?"

"About what," she repeated. "About Linda Kellogg."

"Mrs. Goldstein," I said, still puzzled but becoming a little annoyed, "could we stop playing Twenty Questions and just get down to the nitty-gritty?"

"Sure, tough-guy-private-eye talk you can do," she said accusingly — sounding uncomfortably like my father — "but when it comes to helping a little girl whose husband beats her up and puts her in the hospital —"

"Wait a minute," I said, interrupting her. "Are you telling me that Linda is in the hospital?"

"That's what I said."

"What hospital?" I put my laundry basket down on her machine.

"That one near Atlantic Avenue."

"Long Island College Hospital?"

"That's the one."

"Mrs. Goldstein, will you do my laundry and hold it for me?"

"Are you going to the hospital to try and help her?"

"Yes."

"Then I'll do your laundry, Mister Private Eye. You go and do what you should have done before, give that brute what for."

I wasn't about to give Dan Kellogg "what for," but I did want to talk to Linda Kellogg. I wasn't feeling very good about her at the moment.

Linda Kellogg was sharing a room with three other women, but I pulled the curtain all the way around her bed so we could have some privacy. I was glad not to find her husband there.

"He's at work," she said. "With his new job he can't take that much time off. He said he'd be coming up later on."

"Tell me what happened."

She didn't look too bad, although her face was bruised and swollen so that she had to speak out of one corner of her mouth. Most

20

of the damage had been done to the rib area; he had cracked two of her ribs.

"He came home, and he was angry," she said in a puzzled voice. "I thought he was all over that. I tried to talk to him, but suddenly he was hitting me and telling me to shut up and leave him alone. I couldn't believe it!"

I didn't think that she should have been all that surprised, but I kept that opinion to myself.

"Who called for an ambulance?"

"Dan did."

"And the police?"

"No police," she said, shaking her head.

"Linda, he could have killed you this time —"

"I want to hire you again," she said, interrupting me. "Find out what's making him so angry, Nick . . . please!"

"I'll find out, all right, but I've already been paid and I didn't do the job. This time it's on the house."

She closed her eyes and said, "Thank you." Her last jolt of painkiller was kicking in.

When I left she looked like she was asleep. I wondered idly what she had told the doctors about how she'd received her injuries. I stopped at the nurses' station to ask for Linda's doctor. His name was Geary, and

21

he wasn't available. The nurse said that he'd be making rounds that evening.

As I left the hospital I figured there was only one way I was going to find out what was making Dan Kellogg so angry, and that was to ask the son of a bitch!

4

Dan Kellogg's place of business was on Metropolitan Avenue, in an industrial area of Greenpoint, and I cabbed it there from the hospital.

Greenpoint is a funny section of Brooklyn, because from some parts of the borough, in order to get there, you've got to go into *Queens* and then come back into Brooklyn. My driver, however, simply jumped onto the BQE — the Brooklyn Queens Expressway — and got off at McGuinness Boulevard, which left us just a few blocks from our destination.

Greenpoint is largely industrial, with some neighborhoods made up of single and multiple dwellings. If you're looking for a nice one-family house with a driveway, a yard, a garage, and a picket fence, though, Greenpoint is not the place for you.

When I got to Kellogg's building, there was a sign on the front that said MUELLER BROS. TRUCKING. I went inside and asked someone where I could find Dan Kellogg and they directed me to the dispatcher's booth.

The man in the booth was a burly guy of about thirty, with thick brown hair and a full mustache. It was the first time I had been closer than across the street from Dan Kellogg.

"Kellogg?" I said, leaning my head in the window of the booth.

"Just a sec," he said. He held a short conversation with someone over the radio, then swiveled around to face me and asked, "Can I help you?"

"I'd like to talk to you in private, if you can get relieved."

"Relieved?" he said, laughing. "Mister, you know how many trucks I'm juggling? I can't get just anybody to relieve me, you know. What's it about?"

"It's about your wife, Mr. Kellogg."

"Linda?" he asked, frowning. "You from the hospital?"

"No."

"The cops? What?"

"I'm investigating her . . . accident." There was an implied lie there, but I figured to let him think I was a cop just long enough to get him out of the booth.

His eyes widened and then he licked his lips, wondering if his wife had sicced the cops on him.

24

"There's a lounge down the hall," he said then. "Wait for me there, will you?"

"Sure."

There was another man in the lounge, but as I entered he got up and left. It took Kellogg five minutes to find "just anybody" to relieve him.

"Why are the police interested in my wife's . . . accident?" he asked, sitting next to me on a worn leather sofa. Even though we were alone in the room, he spoke softly. "Did somebody say something . . ."

"About what, Mr. Kellogg?" I asked, prodding him.

"Nothing," he muttered. "What is it you want to know?"

"I want to know exactly how your wife received her injuries."

"Didn't the hospital tell you?"

"I want you to tell me."

"She fell . . . while changing a light bulb."

"Really?"

"Yes . . . really," he said haltingly. "That's what happened."

I stared at him for a few minutes, letting him stew.

"Look . . ." he said nervously, "that's how it happened. Did anybody say different?"

"Can I see your hands, Mr. Kellogg?"

"What for?" he asked, burying his hands in his lap.

"I'm curious," I said. "Humor me."

"Look," he said, standing up and keeping his hands behind him, "I don't know what you're after, but I think I want to see your badge and identification."

"That won't be necessary, Mr. Kellogg," I said, standing up. He was about my height, but he had me by a good twenty pounds across his shoulders and chest. Still, I was pretty sure I could handle him. Men who beat up on women can rarely handle another man. "I'm not a policeman. I never said I was."

"What?" His face turned red. He forgot about his hands and allowed them to come into sight. I could see that he had a couple of skinned knuckles. "Just who the hell are you, mister?"

"Somebody who'd like to know what kind of man would take his anger out on a woman, with his hands," I said, and then added, "and not just any woman, but his own wife."

His hands closed into fists, but he held them at his sides.

"Get out of here!"

"You beat up your wife, Mr. Kellogg," I said, taking out one of my business cards, "you've done it before, only this time you put her in the hospital. You know it and I know it." I tucked one card into his shirt pocket. "I'm going to prove it, and I'm going to find out why — unless you want to tell me that right now. What is it that makes you so angry that you've got to beat up your wife to get rid of the anger?"

"I ain't telling you shit," he said. "I don't have to tell you nothing!"

"You're right about that," I said. "You don't have to tell me anything, so I'll tell you something, Danny. If you touch that girl again, I'm going to personally break you in half."

"You think you can?" he asked, puffing up his chest, but his fists stayed at his sides.

I smiled at him. "I know I can."

He snorted and said, "What are you, her boyfriend?"

"No, Danny boy," I said, quelling the urge to deck him. "Your wife loves you, although God only knows why. She doesn't have a boyfriend, but I wish she did. She needs someone to protect her from you."

"And you're volunteering for the job?"

"That's right, Danny," I said, poking his chest with my right forefinger, "I'm volunteering. You want to talk to me now?"

"I got nothing to say to you! Get out of here before I throw you out."

I laughed in his face, hoping that he

would take a swing at me.

"That's a laugh," I said. "In case you haven't noticed, I'm not a woman, so don't waste your threats on me. Just remember what I said, and if you want to talk to me, just give me a call."

He stood there shaking with impotent rage, and when I was dead sure he wasn't going to swing I left, feeling more than vague disappointment.

5

Two nights later I was returning home, dragging my ass. I had been tailing Kellogg again for the past two days — I decided I'd even try watching him on the weekend — and had still come up empty. I was tired, and very frustrated. I had stopped off for a beer on the way home at Aldretti's, a neighborhood bar, and the one beer had stretched into two during a conversation about horse racing, and then into a third during an argument about which was the better horse, Easy Goer or Sunday Silence, both of which had been recently retired by injuries.

After talking to Kellogg that afternoon two days ago, I had returned to the hospital. I couldn't speak with Linda because she was asleep, but I was able to speak with her doctor.

"In my opinion," Dr. Geary said, "her injuries are not consistent with her story about falling off of a chair while changing a light bulb."

"Are you required to make a report to the

police?" I asked. "I mean, this is not a knife or gunshot wound, I know, but you do suspect violence."

"I didn't say that, Mr. Delvecchio." Dr. Geary was a white-haired, distinguished-looking man in his sixties. He was soft-spoken and had, I suspected, a pleasing bedside manner. He was probably very popular with his patients.

"I do suspect violence," he went on, "but as you say, this is very different from a gunshot wound. I *suspect* violence, but I can't prove it, and I certainly can't prove it was her husband." I hadn't mentioned *domestic* violence. "That is what *you* suspect, isn't it?"

"Yes."

"Well," he said, "I can't help you, Mr. Delvecchio, but I am glad that you are helping her."

"Yeah, well," I said, "I'm doing the best I can, Doctor."

Unfortunately, the best I could do had landed her in the hospital . . .

One room of my four-room apartment is set up as an office, and it has its own entrance from the hall. There was only one other apartment on my floor, the third, and that was Samantha Karson's. I entered

30

through the office door, and my new friend was winking at me from my desk, a red light going on and off, on and off several times. I switched on the light and walked to the desk. I'd only had the telephone answering machine for about a month. It had been a gift from Sam on my birthday. She had bought it secondhand, which was the only way she could have afforded it, but I appreciated the thought. She also thought I should have a computer. I said I couldn't afford one, and she said it would streamline my operation. I laughed. If my "operation" got any more streamlined, the "patient" would die.

I stared at the red light and contemplated not checking the messages until the next morning, but I finally pressed the "play" button and propped my hip on my desk to listen. I didn't care who was on the machine, I wasn't leaving my apartment again tonight. I was going to pop a frozen dinner into the oven and watch a ball game.

The first message was from my father: "You know I hate these machines. I want to talk to someone with a pulse. I want you to come to dinner tomorrow night. Your brother will be here and your sister will be doing the cooking. Call me. I hate these fucking —"

31

The second message was from Walter Koenig, Salvatore Cabretta's attorney. It had been a month since I turned them down, and I'd forgotten about them.

"Mr. Delvecchio, this is Walter Koenig. My number is two-five-seven-three-one-four-two, please call me at your earliest convenience. It is very important that we speak. It would be to our mutual advantage."

Yeah, sure . . .

The third message was from my brother, Father Vinnie.

"Nick, it's Vinnie. No matter what time you get this, call me at the Rectory. It's urgent. The number is two-five-one, three-nine-one-six."

I frowned at the urgency that was present in my brother's voice. Usually, I was the only one who could get him that rattled. Vinnie, two years older than me, was very disapproving of my way of life, and of the way I treated my family. I, on the other hand, was proud of my older brother, the priest — but I'd be damned if I'd ever tell him that.

I picked up the phone and dialed the Rectory number of the Church of the Holy Family in Canarsie. It rang once and was picked up.

"Nick?"

Jesus, I thought, what was he doing, sitting on the phone?

"Vinnie?"

"Wait." He covered the phone with his hand but I heard him say, "No, Monsignor, I have it." Then he came back on the line. "Nick?"

"Vinnie, what's going on —"

"I can't tell you now, Nick, not on the phone. Are you coming to Pop's for dinner tomorrow?"

"Vinnie —"

"I really need to talk to you, Nick," Vinnie said. "It's important!"

It wasn't what he said, but how he was saying it. His voice was actually shaking.

"All right, Vinnie," I said. "I'll see you at Pop's tomorrow."

"Great!" he said. "Nick . . . thanks for this."

"Sure, Vin. See you tomorrow."

He hung up without saying good night, or even a "God bless you."

Man, something was *wrong!*

I waited until the next morning to call my father to tell him that I would be over for dinner.

My father reacted in what was becoming typical Vito Delvecchio fashion.

"It's about fuckin' time."

6

When I reached my father's house, Maria was already there, but Vinnie hadn't arrived yet. I had tailed Dan Kellogg home and then hopped the subway and come straight to Pop's house.

I got a hug and a kiss and a "Why haven't you called" from my pretty sister. I ducked the last one. My sister, since her divorce, lived near my father in a small apartment. Even she couldn't live *with* him, though, not at this stage of his life.

I wasn't being biased when I referred to my sister as pretty. She had always been pretty, and the boys had started chasing her at an early age. She had always worn her brown hair long, and it was beautiful hair, like my mother's had been when she was young. Of course, Maria's older brothers had always been very protective of her, and she both loved and hated us for it.

In retirement, my father had regressed to the point where he was more little boy than I or my brothers had ever been. He wasn't senile, he just wanted what he wanted, and he couldn't have it, so he reacted by cursing and drinking beer . . .

What my old man wanted more than anything else, even seventeen years after the fact, was my older brother Joey back. Private First Class Joseph Delvecchio was killed in Vietnam when he was nineteen. A soldier walking next to him stepped on a mine, and it killed both of them.

At least there had been enough left of Joey to send home. The funeral had been a phenomenon to me. Eight hundred people, touched by Joey in his nineteen years of life, came to the funeral parlor over a three-day period, to the amazement of everyone concerned.

At the time Vinnie was seventeen and I was fifteen. Maria had been five, and she stuck close to me throughout the wake and funeral. She claimed she could still remember the whole thing vividly. She remembered Joey, too, and I was glad of that. Everybody who knew Joey remembered him, but unlike my father, we had all let him go to his rest.

Pop had Joey's picture on the wall, above a statue of the Virgin Mother, like a little shrine to his memory. I hated the damned thing. I didn't need a shrine to remember my brother. I loved him — and still love him

— but I hated what his death had done to my father. It had turned him bitter, more bitter even than the death of my mother, who died of cancer the year before Joey. Maybe it was a combination of the two. Who knew? At least he hadn't erected a shrine to my mother. He had let her go to her rest; why couldn't he do the same thing for Joey?

I wanted my father to get on with his life. There *was* life after retirement from the docks, but try to tell him that.

"Where's Father Vinnie?" I asked Maria.

"He's coming, Nick." She squeezed my hand and said, "I'm so glad you're here."

I put my other hand over hers and said, "What's the matter, Maria? Some boy bothering you? You want me to beat him up?"

She laughed and said, "I'm well beyond that, Nicky. No, I'm worried about Father Vinnie."

"Why?"

"I don't know, but something feels wrong."

"Woman's intuition?"

"It hasn't done me much good to this point, has it?" The irony was plain in her voice.

My sister was twenty-two, and had made a few mistakes in her life. One was her marriage, which had broken up last year, right after she and all the other passengers had been rescued from a hijacked plane. That time was the most helpless I'd ever felt in my life, but I'll say one thing for the experience. She seemed to have grown as a result of it. The rest of us just "aged," but bless her heart, she'd grown — and she had proved it by getting rid of her husband, "Numbnuts," otherwise known as Peter Geller.

Of course, Father Vinnie had not been happy when she married out of "our faith," but even he was happy when she divorced Geller — although Vinnie would never let the Church know that. His happiness for her was that of a brother for his sister. Of course, as a priest he could not condone divorce.

"Has he said anything to you?"

"No," she said, "but he sounded funny when I talked to him yesterday. Have you talked to him lately?"

"No," I lied. I decided to keep Vinnie's late-night phone call to myself. I sniffed the air and changed the subject. "The sauce smells good. Yours?"

"Uh-huh," she said. "I'm making lasagne and veal parmigiana."

"Umm," I said, licking my lips. The only thing I liked better was spaghetti with garlic and olive oil.

"Speaking of which," she said, sliding her hand from mine, "I'd better get to it. You want a beer?"

"Sure. Where's Pop?"

"In his room."

Pop's "room" was a room that he had added on to the house himself when we were kids. He had a desk, a recliner, and a TV in there, and that's where he used to go to hide from all of us.

Maria handed me a Bud and I carried it into my father's room.

"Hello, Pop."

He was seated in his recliner, watching the news on TV.

"Humph," he said, "big-shot private eye made time for his old man, huh?"

"Pop —"

"Okay, never mind," he said, "you're here; I guess I should be grateful."

"You want a beer, Pop?" I asked.

He raised his left hand and there was a half-consumed bottle of Bud already in it.

"I'm gonna see if Maria needs any help."

"Your sister takes after your mother in the kitchen," Pop said, "she don't need your help. Sit down."

I went and sat behind his desk. It was the only other place to sit in the room.

He hadn't shaved, and his stubble was gray. I always lose track of his birthdays, but I'm pretty sure he is sixty or better. Maria knows all our birthdays, and she never forgets them. We don't celebrate Joey's, but she always lets us know when it's here.

My father had put on weight since his retirement. He could have worked until he was sixty-two, but his back had started to give him trouble when he got into his late forties, and had finally driven him to a disability retirement at fifty-five or so. His belly hung over his belt, a testament to all the beer he'd consumed since retiring, but his biceps were still hard, even though there was some loosening of the skin around them. I frowned. It was the first time I had noticed the loose skin. I stared at my father and wondered when he had started to look so old. His face was naturally red, his hair — worn in a Mickey Spillane crew cut — was totally gray, and his eyes were unnaturally red. I wondered what time he'd started drinking today.

"Got a girl yet?" he asked.

"No, Pop."

"Making money?"

"No, Pop."

"Ready to try some other line of work?"

"No, Pop."

Pop hadn't liked it when I became a cop. The Irish became cops, he'd said, Italians became priests — or wise guys. When I left the cops and got a PI's license, he had liked that even less.

He shook his head wearily and said, "If Joey was alive . . ."

"I'm glad we had this little talk, Pop," I said, rising quickly, "but I think I hear Vinnie." I rushed from the room and went into the kitchen to join Maria.

"Nick?" she said, eyeing me.

"He started that 'If Joey was alive' stuff," I said. "I had to get out of there."

"Be patient, Nick."

"Maria, baby sister . . ." I started, but we both heard the front door open and close.

"Father Vinnie," she said.

"I'll get him," I said. "Gimme another beer."

I went into the living room and found my brother in front of the Virgin, looking up at the picture of Joey. He wasn't wearing his priest's collar tonight. He had an odd look on his face, one I didn't remember ever having seen before. When you grow up with someone, you eventually see every facial expression that person has — happy, sad,

40

mad, scared — sure, I'd seen my brother scared before, but this was different.

This was naked fear.

"Vinnie?"

Without looking at me he said, "You ever wonder what he'd be doing if he was alive today?"

"Same thing we do," I said, "try to avoid coming to see Pop too often."

Normally, that would have drawn a disapproving look, or a verbal scolding from Father Vinnie, but he let it go right by.

Oh boy, I thought, something *was* wrong.

"The monsignor catch you whacking off in the confessional or something?" I wanted to ask, but bit my tongue. If this was serious, he was going to have to get to it in his own time.

"If he was here," I said, "we could all go out and tie one on together."

"Yeah," Vinnie said, and he smiled. I knew what he was remembering — the first time the three of us had gotten into a bottle of Pop's bourbon. We'd gotten so sick that Pop hadn't even pounded us. I think that was why I hardly ever drank anything but beer.

"You guys," I said, moving next to him, "you almost got me killed that time."

"It was your idea."

41

"Hell it was," I said. "I was the baby, remember?"

"Some baby," Vinnie said, "you thought of things Joey and I would never had thought of."

I looked up at the picture of my brother Joey. It was taken just before he'd gone to 'Nam.

"You think he'd be a priest now too?" I asked.

"Him?" Vinnie said. "He'd be a bishop by now."

"Or a cardinal."

We looked at each other and we both said, "Or Pope."

That got a chuckle from him, but it didn't go a long way.

My brother was taller than me, six-two, and better-looking. If I had his looks I wouldn't have become a priest, I would have terrorized the female population of New York — and they would have loved every minute of it.

"Here," I said, handing him the other beer. As he took it I said, "You want to talk, Vinnie?"

He looked beyond me, toward the kitchen, toward Pop's room.

"After dinner, Nick, when we're alone, okay?"

"Whenever you're ready, big brother."

Maria entered the room at that point, said, "Father Vinnie," and gave him the same hug, kiss, and question she'd given me.

Pretty, my sister Maria, but not a lot of imagination.

7

My father's house was a one-family brick house on Ovington Avenue. If you looked at a map of Brooklyn you'd see the area marked "Borough Park," but we always called it Bensonhurst. What you call it depends on when and where you were brought up.

Most of the conversation at dinner was between Maria and my father. I chimed in once in a while, but Father Vinnie was silent the whole time, pushing his food around his plate.

"Aye," my father said at one point, "Father, what'samatta, they feed you this good in the Rectory every day?"

"No, Pop," Vinnie said, "the only time I get food this good is when you or Maria cook."

"So what'samatta, you're not eating?"

"I guess I'm just not hungry."

"Well, pass your plate over here, then," Pop said. "I ain't about to let good food go to waste."

Maria stood up and started to clear the table.

"I'll help . . ." Father Vinnie started, but Maria cut him off and showed me that she was more on the ball than I gave her credit for.

"Never mind, Vinnie," she said. "You'll just get in the way. Why don't you and Nicky go for a walk? By the time you get back I'll have coffee ready."

Vinnie looked at me and I said, "It sounds like a good idea to me. Come on, Vin."

The house was between Fourteenth and Fifteenth Avenues, and when we left the house we started walking toward Fifteenth, just strolling.

"What's going on, man?" I asked my brother. "I've never seen you like this."

He rubbed his hand over his face and said, "I don't know where to start."

"It's a cliché, Vin, but start at the beginning, why don't you?"

"Yeah," Vinnie said, "the beginning. That was this past Saturday."

This was Monday.

"What happened Saturday?"

"The police came to church Saturday," he said, looking down at the ground while we walked.

"Is that a first for the Church of the Holy Family?"

"It is for me," Vinnie said. "I was hearing

45

confessions and they took me right out of the confessional. Monsignor Genovese had to finish up for me."

"Why? I mean, why'd they pull you out of church?"

"They took me to the precinct, Nick."

"What for?"

"It seems one of my parishioners was killed Thursday night."

"So? What's that got to do with you?"

He looked at me then and I saw the fear in his eyes.

"They think I killed her."

I grabbed his arm and turned him around to face me. There was fear in his eyes, and something else. Pain. "What? Say that again?"

"They think I killed her, Nick."

"That's crazy. Did they say that?"

"No, not in so many words."

I took my hand off his arm and we started walking again.

"So? Talk to me, Vinnie. What'd they ask you?"

"They asked me how well I knew her," Vinnie said. "They asked me if I ever saw her outside of church. Nicky, they think I was her . . . lover, or something."

"Wait a minute, Vinnie, this is getting screwier by the second." I grabbed his arm again and stopped him. "Why didn't you call me?"

"I wasn't under arrest or anything," Vinnie said. "They just said they wanted to talk to me. They didn't tell me what it was about until we got to the precinct."

"The six-nine?" The Sixty-ninth Precinct was the local precinct in Canarsie, where the church was located.

"Yes. When we got there they told me that Gloria — that was her name, Gloria Mancuso — that she was dead, and asked me what I knew about her and her husband. Then they started asking me the other questions . . . the . . . the suggestive ones."

"Wait a minute. She was married, and they think she was having an affair with you, a priest?"

"That's the impression I got from their questions," Vinnie said. "God, Nick, I'm scared. I wasn't so scared then, but the more I think about it, the more scared I get. What's the monsignor going to think?"

"What does he know, so far?"

"Just that one of our parishioners was killed, and that the police asked me questions about her. He wanted to complain to the police about the detectives pulling me out of confession, but I stopped him."

"Why?"

"I don't want him to know what they're thinking until it's absolutely necessary."

I put my hand on his shoulder and said, "Vinnie, I'm your brother, but I gotta ask you. You weren't seeing her, were you?"

When he didn't answer right away I got a cold feeling in the pit of my stomach.

"Vinnie . . ."

He moved away from me then, turned his back and walked to the curb.

"Come on, Vinnie!"

He looked at me over his shoulder. He had the same look he had on his face when, at six and eight years of age, we had broken one of Mom's favorite lamps by playing ball in the house.

"I think I wanted to, Nick."

"But did you?"

"I never slept with her, if that's what you're thinking," he said, "but . . . I did . . . I did see her outside of church a few times."

"Why, Vinnie?"

"She was an attractive woman, Nick," Vinnie said. "I mean, she was beautiful, and she was always . . . flirting with me. One night she called me and asked me to meet her. I thought she was in trouble."

"And?"

"I met her at a diner, and we had some

48

coffee. She told me then that she was . . . attracted to me."

I could understand that. After all, my brother was a good-looking guy, even if he was a priest.

"What did you do?"

He laughed humorlessly and said, "I ran. God, I got out of that diner fast. The following Sunday she was laughing at me in church."

"And after that?"

He turned and faced me.

"Nick, I swear to God, I only saw her two more times after that."

"Where?"

"She invited me to a party at her house."

"And you went?"

"The monsignor wanted me to go. Her husband is well off, and he donates time and money to the parish. Monsignor Genovese wanted to keep him happy."

Church politics, I thought.

"And what happened?"

"I only intended to stay a short time, but somehow she managed to get me alone, even though I was avoiding her."

"This broad sounds like she had all the moves." Naturally, my brother would never know how to handle a sharp cookie like Gloria Mancuso.

"She said she . . . she wanted to have sex with me. I tried to talk her out of it, but she said it was no use. She wanted me, and she was going to have me."

Every man's dream — unless he was wearing a priest's collar.

"Nick," he said helplessly, "I didn't know what to do. I don't have any . . . experience dealing with that kind of woman."

"And the other time you saw her?"

He composed himself and continued.

"She called one night and asked me to come to that Holiday Inn in Staten Island."

"Staten Island? And you went?"

"She — she said she'd kill herself if I didn't meet her."

"Jesus, Vinnie . . ." I started, then decided that was too harsh. I composed *myself* and then said, "Vinnie, this broad sounds crazy. You, uh, went?"

"I went," he said, shaking his head. "Nick, I couldn't take the chance . . . She had taken a room and I . . . sneaked up. God," he said, looking at the sky. "I felt so . . . dirty, like I was doing something wrong."

"You weren't, you know," I said. "She was."

"Yeah," he said, putting his hand to his forehead, "I know, Nick."

"What happened?"

"She let me into the room. She was wearing a nightgown, and some kind of perfume . . . Nick, she was beautiful, and I *am* a man, after all."

"Vinnie . . ."

"She took off the nightgown and taunted me, standing there naked and . . . and so beautiful. Oh, Nick," he said in an anguished tone, "I wanted to . . . I wanted to so badly . . ."

"But . . . you didn't."

"I told her no, I couldn't break my vows."

"What did she say?"

He bit his lip and I could see that his hands were shaking.

"She . . . pressed her body against me. I . . . I couldn't move. I felt as if my feet had taken root. My body was . . . betraying me."

I knew what he meant. Just listening to him tell it, my body was betraying *me.*

"She said if I didn't make . . . love to her, she would tell her husband that . . . that I raped her."

"Jesus, what did you do?"

"I told her I forgave her," Vinnie said, "and I left. She was screaming something about making sure I would pay, but I didn't listen . . . I left."

"And she never told her husband the lie?"

"I guess not."

"When was the last time you saw her, Vinnie?"

He looked at the ground, scuffing his shoes.

"Vinnie?"

"That was Thursday night, Nick."

It was getting worse.

"Vinnie, you saw her that Thursday night, and after you saw her, someone killed her?"

"Yes."

"Where?"

"In that motel."

"Jesus . . . Did you tell the police you were with her?"

He stared at me, tears forming in his eyes, and said, "God forgive me, no, I didn't, Nick. I didn't . . . I lied . . ."

"You didn't lie, Vinnie," I said, "you just didn't tell them you were there. Did they ask you if you were there?"

"No, not specifically —"

"Then you didn't lie."

"It's like a lie, Nick," Vinnie said, "don't try to convince me otherwise."

"Vinnie," I said, "why aren't you wearing your collar?"

His hand went to his throat, as if he'd forgotten he wasn't wearing it.

"I — I can't —" he stammered, "I don't deserve —"

"Vinnie," I said, moving closer to him, "what do you want me to do?"

He stared at me, naked fear in his eyes, and said, "I want you to help me, Nick . . . Oh, God, I want you to help me . . ."

For the first time since I can remember I put my arms around my brother.

"That's just what I'm gonna do, Vinnie, don't worry. That's what I'm gonna do."

8

On the way back to the house we decided to keep this from the rest of the family as long as possible. Maria kept giving me looks over coffee. She assumed that I had found out what was troubling Vinnie during our walk, and she expected me to tell her. Her assumption was, of course, correct, but her expectations were denied her when I was the first to leave. I told them I had some late work to do on a case, and Vinnie walked me to the door so that Maria wouldn't.

"I'll call you tomorrow, Nick," Maria said firmly.

That was fine with me. I had the answering machine.

At the door I told Vinnie, "Don't say anything to anyone until we talk again. Understand?"

"I understand," Vinnie said. "What are you going to do?"

"I'm gonna check into this," I said. "What were the detectives' names?"

"Uh, Devlin and O'Neal."

I didn't know them.

"I'll talk to them first, and then go out to Staten Island and see what I can find out."

"Nick," Vinnie said urgently, "if I get arrested —"

"If you get arrested —" I started, and then stopped. I had been about to tell him not to worry about it, but that was wrong. We had to deal with the possibility that he might be arrested.

"Let's step outside," I said, and we did, closing the door behind us. "I'm going to talk to the cops tomorrow. After that, if I think you need a lawyer, I'll get you one. Did they read you your rights?"

"No, but —"

"That's right, you weren't under arrest. Look, just don't go anywhere tomorrow. I'll come by the Rectory. Okay?"

"What time?"

"I don't know," I said, "after I see the detectives. First I've got to find somebody who knows them, so that they'll talk to me. Just wait for me."

"All right," he said. "I may not be in the Rectory, but I'll be on the church and school grounds."

"Okay, okay," I said. "I'll see you tomorrow."

"Nick," he said, "uh . . . thanks."

"Don't be an ass."

★ ★ ★

When I got home I went into my office and sat behind my desk. My head was still spinning from what my brother had told me. How could anyone think that Vinnie, a priest, would kill someone? That was a dumb question even for me to ask myself. Anyone was capable of murder. As far as the cops were concerned, Vinnie was just a man, just another suspect. Jesus, I thought, this Gloria must have been really something to have my brother going around in circles. I had always thought that Father Vinnie was immune to women. That showed that I didn't know my brother as well as I thought I did. Maybe that came from not spending enough time with him.

Jesus, now I was starting to sound like my father.

I had to put my house in order before I could work on my brother's case. I needed someone to follow Dan Kellogg for me. I thought of a couple of amateurs I could have asked. There was my friend Hacker, a computer genius who lived in Park Slope, but if I took him out from behind his computer, he would probably get lost. I dismissed a couple of other choices, too, and decided to ask another PI.

I picked up the phone and dialed Miles

Jacoby's number. Jack lived in Manhattan, but I didn't think he'd mind coming across the river for a favor.

"Jacoby."

"Hello, Jack. It's Nick Delvecchio."

"How're you doing, Nick?"

"I could be better," I said. "I need a favor."

"Shoot."

I told him about the Kellogg case, from beginning to end.

"Sounds pretty straightforward," he said. "What are you working on?"

"Something personal," I said, "real personal. I can't get into it right now, but if you're not busy —"

"Say no more, buddy," Jack said, cutting me off, "I'll pick Kellogg up at his house in the morning."

"That'll be pretty early, Jack," I said, trying to make it easier on him. "Why not pick him up at work?"

"If he stops off somewhere on the way to work and tears off a piece, and you miss it, you're gonna kick yourself, Nick."

I knew that.

"Besides, I'm up early for roadwork, anyway."

Jack used to box pro.

"You getting' back into it?" I asked.

"No, just keepin' in shape. I'll report in to you tomorrow night. Okay?"

"I appreciate this, Jack," I said. "I'll just turn the fee around to you and —"

"We can talk about that later," he said. "Good luck with your personal thing. If I can help, let me know."

"You are helping. Thanks, Jack."

So, that took care of Dan Kellogg. I looked at my watch. It was too late for me to call the cop I wanted to call. I'd have to try and get him early in the morning. If anyone could help me in getting Detectives Devlin and O'Neal to talk to me, he could.

I shut off the desk lamp and left the office. As I was making coffee, I thought, jeez, Devlin and O'Neal. Just like Pop said. The Irish became cops.

9

I had been to the Sixty-ninth Precinct before, but not for years. When I was still in uniform — or "in the bag," as cops say — I was loaned out to them once or twice. When I entered, though, I didn't see anyone I knew. There was such a turnover of personnel at police precincts, that being out of the job for almost five years just about put me out of touch.

I approached the front desk and told the sergeant there that I would like to see Detective Devlin and/or Detective O'Neal.

"What's it about?" he asked without looking at me.

"Homicide."

"Old or new?"

"What?"

He looked at me now.

"An old case, or a new one?"

"A current one."

"You a witness?"

I took out my ID and passed it to him. He looked at it, then passed it back to me.

"Wait a second."

He picked up the phone, punched a few

buttons, and waited.

"Yeah, Devlin or O'Neal . . . Yeah, I got a PI down here named Delvecchio. Wants to see one of you about a current homicide case . . . uh-huh . . . okay, sure . . ."

He hung up and said, "Upstairs to the second floor."

"Thanks."

He didn't reply.

I took the stairs to the second floor and when I reached the top there was a man waiting for me there. He was tall, with narrow shoulders and a burgeoning girth, graying hair and long legs. He looked like a twenty-year man. He was wearing a white shirt with an open collar, gold-colored pants, and he had both hands in his pocket.

"Delvecchio?"

"That's right."

"Follow me," he said curtly. No handshake, no introduction. I didn't even know if he was Devlin or O'Neal.

I followed him to a door with a sign on the wall that said "P.D.U." It stood for Precinct Detective Unit.

Inside were a number of desks, half full and half empty. At the back of the room was a holding pen. The walls were painted a drab green. He led me to two desks in the back of the room that were butted up against one another. There was a man sitting at one desk holding a Styrofoam cup of coffee. There was another cup on the empty desk. The seated man was sandy-haired and overweight. Another twenty-year man. Two old war horses paired off with each other. This wasn't going to be easy.

"Mr. Delvecchio, this is my partner, Detective O'Neal." This was said by the man who had waited for me by the stairs.

"I guess that makes you Detective Devlin."

"Hey," Devlin said, "you *are* a detective."

Nope, I thought, not going to be easy at all.

Devlin sat down and picked up his coffee. "So?" he said.

I was a little off balance. This wasn't exactly the reception I had expected, I guess.

"I'm here about the Gloria Mancuso case."

Devlin looked across the expanse of both desks at his partner and said, "Mancuso?"

"Not our case."

Devlin looked at me and said, "Not our case. Sorry."

"Look, I know it's not your case," I said. "I know she was killed in Staten Island, but —"

"Then why don't you go to Staten Island

and harass them?" Devlin asked.

"Hey, I'm not harassing anybody," I said, wondering what was going on. "I'm just trying to get some information."

"About what?" Devlin asked.

"Look, you guys pulled my brother in here on Sunday and questioned him. I want to know if he's a suspect."

"Your brother?" Devlin said.

"The priest," O'Neal said. "His brother is the priest."

"Oh," Devlin said. "That's nice, your brother's a priest."

"Yeah," I said, starting to heat up, "he's a priest and I used to be a cop. All I'm asking for here is some cooperation."

"You used to be on the job, huh?" Devlin said.

"That's right."

"What happened?"

"I busted one too many heads," I said. "What's your problem, Devlin?"

"Since you ask," Devlin said, setting the coffee down on the desk, "I'll tell you what my problem is. I don't like getting called into my CO's office and being told that I got to cooperate with some two-bit PI who used to be on the job, when the ex-cop PI don't have enough sense to come right to me with his request."

"Oh," I said, "I see."

"Yeah," Devlin said. He picked his coffee up, sat back in his chair, and stared at me.

"I fucked up."

"Royally," O'Neal said.

I had called an old colleague of mine, Deputy Inspector Ed Gorman, who had been my "rabbi" when I was on the job. It was he who had worked out the deal for me where I could retire on a one-third disability instead of facing criminal charges. I figured if anyone would know these two detectives, he might. He said he'd take care of it. Obviously he didn't know them, but he had called their CO and asked for cooperation. When they in turn had been called in by their captain, they had been "told" to cooperate, not "asked."

"Okay," I said, "I fucked up, I'm sorry. Obviously, what I wanted to happen did not."

"And it ain't gonna," Devlin said. "We were told to cooperate and we will. We will talk to you about any of our cases you want to hear about. We can't talk to you about a case that isn't ours."

"Look," I said, "give me a chance to clear this up. I didn't know you fellas, so I called a friend of mine and asked if he did. He said he'd help."

"A friend?" Devlin asked.

"A DI."

He mugged and looked at his friend.

"I wish I had a friend who was a deputy inspector." He looked at me again and asked, "Why couldn't he help you out with your, uh, departmental difficulties?"

"He did," I said. "He kept me out of jail."

That surprised them, and they exchanged a glance that they had probably been exchanging for years.

"Sounds like a nice man to have on your side," Devlin said carefully.

I smelled a deal in the air, but I figured they wanted me to approach them with it.

"Okay," I said, "my rabbi is your rabbi. What have you got?"

They exchanged a glance again, and O'Neal nodded.

"Okay," Devlin said, looking around quickly. "We got a call from a Detective Lacy at the one-two-two in Staten Island. They had a homicide at a Holiday Inn on Richmond Avenue. A broad was killed in one of the rooms."

"How?"

"She was strangled."

"Okay, go ahead."

"They wanted us to pick up a priest named . . ." Here he looked at his partner.

"He knows his name," O'Neal said, "it's his fuckin' brother, for Chrissake."

"Right," Devlin said. "They wanted us to pick up your brother and question him."

"They weren't at the, uh, interview?"

"No," Devlin said, "they said they would talk to him later."

"They wanted you to soften him up first. Scare him a little."

"Put the fear of God into him, they said," O'Neal said, chuckling. When he saw I wasn't laughing he stopped and said, "Well, they thought it was funny."

"So you pulled him out of church right in the middle of confession, hauled him back here, and questioned him."

"Right."

"And some of the questions were . . . suggestive."

"Huh?"

"You made him believe that you thought he was sleeping with the woman."

"Right," Devlin said. "Personally, I didn't like doing it. I mean, Jesus Christ, the guy's a priest!"

I looked at O'Neal but he didn't comment. I guess he didn't mind doing it. No Catholic guilt there.

"Do they have anything solid on my brother?"

65

They looked at each other again.

"We really don't know," Devlin said. "We were just cooperating, you know? Precinct to precinct?"

"Yeah," I said, "I know, but if you had to guess . . ."

I looked at Devlin, and then at O'Neal. It was O'Neal who answered.

"If I had to guess," he said, "I'd tell you to get your brother a good lawyer."

10

A very attractive woman in her twenties answered the door at the Rectory. I had only been there once or twice, so I didn't know if she was regular help or volunteer. She had short brown hair, pretty eyes, and a nice mouth. She was wearing a blouse and skirt, and she had nice, trim legs that would have been shown off better if she hadn't been wearing sensible shoes.

The precinct was located on Rockaway Parkway and Foster Avenue. The Church of the Holy Family was located on Rockaway Parkway and Flatlands Avenue. The distance was about four long blocks, and I'd walked it.

"Can I help you?" she asked.

"Yes, I'd like to see Father Vin— uh, Father Delvecchio."

"Are you a parishioner?"

"No, ma'am, I'm his brother."

She smiled and said, "Oh. Well, Father is in the school gymnasium. The regular gym teacher is ill, and Father is taking his class."

"Thank you, ma'am."

"Sister," she said, "Sister Olivia."

"Really?" I said. Boy, you can't tell these days, when they don't have to wear habits.

"Thank you . . . Sister."

"You're very welcome."

She closed the door and I stood there shaking my head. They shouldn't allow nuns to look like that. Sister Olivia looked nothing like my seventh-grade teacher, Sister Manassa Mauler.

The School of the Holy Family was across the courtyard from the church. I knew from the other times I had been there that the best entrance for the gym was on the Conklin Avenue side. I walked through the courtyard to that side of the building and entered. Once inside I had only to follow the sounds of the whistle and the slapping feet.

As I entered the gym I saw Vinnie. He was wearing a T-shirt with the school insignia on his chest, which precluded him from wearing his collar. The kids running back and forth with a basketball looked like eleven- or twelve-year-old boys and girls. The school was a boys-and-girls parochial school, grades kindergarten to eight.

I caught myself watching one of the girls who was running up and down the floor. She had long, flowing blond hair, beautiful skin, strong legs and thighs, and she needed some sort of athletic bra. The boys her age, running with her, were more interested in her bouncing boobs than the bouncing ball. Some of the other girls were pretty, too, and somewhat advanced physically, but the blonde was a total knockout.

Jesus, I thought, they didn't have nuns *or* students like this when I was in parochial school.

Vinnie saw me and held up five fingers, indicating that there was five minutes left in the class. I spent the five minutes watching that blond girl run up and down the floor and trying not to feel guilty about it.

Vinnie finally blew the whistle and told the boys and girls to go and get dressed. They filed out through a door at the opposite end of the gym.

"Hi, Nick." He was wiping his hands on a white towel he'd had around his neck.

"Sister Olivia told me you were over here. How come they didn't have nuns like her when we were kids?"

"They have changed, haven't they?"

"So have the kids," I said, "especially the girls."

"You noticed Lisa."

"The blonde? I couldn't help it. What grade is she in, anyway?"

"Eighth," Vinnie said. "She's thirteen."

"My God," I said. "Her mother ought to talk to her about a sports bra before she starts high school."

"She can't," he said, wiping his dripping face with the towel. "Her mother was Gloria Mancuso."

"Oh." I wasn't sure what to say. "At least that explains her looks."

"Oh, she's got her mother's looks, all right," he said, "and her attitude as well. She's gonna be a terror in high school."

I could just imagine how many teenage boys would be walking the halls of her high school with swollen balls.

"Let me just check on the kids," he said, "and then you can walk me to the Rectory. I've got to take a shower. That was the only gym class I had to take. The others are covered."

I thought how ironic it was that he'd had to take the class that Gloria Mancuso's daughter was in.

"I'm surprised she's in school," I commented.

"First day back since her mother . . . died."

"When are they burying her?"

"I'm not sure."

He used his key to open a side door of the Rectory, and I followed him up a flight of

70

back stairs to his room. I'd seen my brother's room only once before, and it hadn't changed. It was still a spare, neat room with a desk, a bed, a chair, and an end table with a lamp. There was also a small bookcase, filled with paperbacks.

"I'll take a quick shower," he said, "and then we'll talk."

When I was a kid I served as an altar boy, so I had seen the inside of a Rectory then. I remember thinking what a hardship it must have been for all the priests to have to share a bathroom. My brother did not have that hardship. He had a bathroom adjoining his room.

I heard the shower go on and checked out the books in the bookcase. There were some fiction and nonfiction best-sellers, some Andrew Greeley books, some of the Harry Kemelman Rabbi books, and some books by William X. Kienzle. The Greeley, Kemelman, and Kienzle books were all mysteries with a clerical detective. I hadn't known that my brother was into mysteries. I moved some of them around and found a book set crosswise atop them. When I took it out I was surprised to find one of Samantha's Kit Karson romances. The lurid cover had been torn off and discarded.

Vinnie reentered the room, wearing a pair

of jockey shorts and drying his hair. He stopped when he saw me in front of the bookcase.

"Sam will be flattered," I said, holding her book up. "What happened to the cover?"

"I bought it in a used-books store like that," he said. "She's a good writer."

"I'll tell her you said so."

"Anything happening with you and her?"

I put her book back where I'd gotten it from and said, "We're friends, Vinnie."

"She was real helpful last year, when Maria was . . . in trouble."

"She's a helpful gal."

"Pop liked her a lot," he said, "I thought maybe you two —"

"Vinnie."

"Okay," he said, "sorry." He went back into the bathroom and came out without the towel. He pulled on a pair of black pants, and then sat on his bed to pull on a pair of black loafers.

"So tell me," he said, "did you talk to the detectives? Do I need a lawyer?"

"Yes, I spoke with them, but I don't know yet if you need a lawyer."

"What do you mean? What did they say?"

"They said they were just assisting the Staten Island detectives with their case. They have no facts themselves, because it's not their case. They were simply asked to question you and . . . shake you up a bit."

"Well, they did that." He stood up, crossed the room and took a white T-shirt from a dresser drawer. He rolled it up, pulled it over his head, and rolled it down.

"The Staten Island detectives will probably be talking to you," I said. "Before that happens, I'll talk to them, but I think I'll find you a lawyer, anyway. I don't know if you need him, but I think you should call him whenever they approach you to speak with you."

He took a new white shirt out of another drawer, stripped the wrapper, and started removing the pins.

"Can't that be avoided for a while?"

"What? Calling the attorney?"

"As soon as I notify the Diocese that I need an attorney, the whole story will have to come out."

"No, it won't."

"The Church will have to foot the bill," Vinnie said. "I'll have to tell them why."

"You tell them you can't talk to them until you speak to your lawyer."

"That's a Catch Twenty-two, Nick," he said, gesturing with the shirt. "I can't tell them why I need a lawyer until I have a lawyer, and they won't hire a lawyer until I tell them why I need one."

"If the Church won't hire you a lawyer," I said, "I'll foot the bill."

"Nick —"

"I'll go with you."

"What?"

"We'll go and talk to whoever we have to talk to together."

"We'll have to go to the office of the Diocese in downtown Brooklyn," he said, "but eventually we're going to have to talk with Manhattan."

"O'Malley himself?" I asked. Cardinal O'Malley was a famous man. He had a fabulous physical presence, which came across well on TV. He always said Midnight Mass on television on Christmas Eve.

"He's going to have to be told."

"Let's take one step at a time," I said. "I'll go to Staten Island to talk to the detective, then I'll get the lawyer and we'll have dinner together. After that, we do what he tells us."

"I can't pay a lawyer —"

"I doubt that we'll have to front any money."

"Look, Nick, it's bad enough that I'm asking you for favors, but to ask your friends —"

"Don't worry about it, Vinnie."

He stared at me for a few moments, then

slipped into the shirt. He tucked it into his pants, then grabbed a black jacket and went to the door. He opened it, but I pressed my palm to the door and closed it again.

"What?" he said.

"Where's your collar, Vinnie?"

"My collar?"

"Your collar."

"Why do you want my collar?"

"Don't play games with me, Father," I said. "I don't want your collar."

"Then why did you ask me for it?"

"Where is it?"

"It's in my jacket pocket."

"Take it out and put it on."

"Nick . . ." he said, starting to open the door, but I kept my palm pressed to it.

"Nick . . ."

"We're going to keep this thing between us as long as we can," I said. "Maybe we'll be able to straighten it out, and maybe we won't, I don't know, but you're going to wear your collar."

He took it out of his pocket and looked at it.

"I don't deserve to."

"Bunk!"

"What?"

"I can't say what I wanted to say, I'm in the presence of a priest."

"I'm not worthy of —"

"Bull dooky!"

"Nick!"

"I'm gonna run out of substitutes pretty soon."

"This is silly —"

"Put the damn collar on!"

"Don't curse in here."

"Then put it on."

My brother stared at me for a few heartbeats and then put the collar on.

"Can I go to work now?" he asked.

I opened the door for him and said, "We'll both go to work now."

11

I played it differently with the Staten Island detectives. Instead of asking Inspector Gorman to call them, I asked Devlin if he would. He did, and Detective Lacy and his partner, Detective Giambone, were expecting me. Before I left the six-nine, O'Neal made a point of reminding me of our little deal. I gave them each one of my business cards and told them that if they ever needed anything to call me. What was implied there was that they should not call Deputy Inspector Gorman directly. Devlin gave me a conspiratorial wink before I left, as if to let me know that we were now all on the same side — theirs!

I borrowed Hacker's 1976 Grand Prix for the ride out to Staten Island. Since he rarely left his computer consoles, it was very unlikely he'd miss it. I decided to stop in and see the detectives before I went by the Holiday Inn, as a courtesy. I'd learned my lesson from fucking up with the six-nine detectives. I wasn't going to make the same mistake with the one-two-two dicks.

I entered the new-looking one-two-two building on Hylan Boulevard. The damned thing looked more like a catering hall than a precinct. I approached the front desk as I had in Brooklyn, and asked for Detectives Lacy and Giambone. The location was changed, but the personnel almost seemed interchangeable. The desk officer called upstairs, announced me, and then told me to go ahead up.

No one was waiting for me at the stairs when I got to the second floor, but I managed to locate the squad room and ask for Lacy and Giambone. I was pointed in Lacy's direction, and told that Giambone was out.

I approached Detective Lacy's desk and he stood up and extended his hand. He looked to be about thirty, nattily attired in a powder-blue suit, his styled hair perfectly in place. I wondered what Devlin and O'Neal would think if they saw Lacy. The new breed of detective.

There were an "out" box and an "in" box on Lacy's desk. His "in" box was empty. His "out" box had a *Wall Street Journal* folded on top of a bunch of blue DD 5s. Apparently, Detective Lacy kept well up on his Detective Follow-Up Reports.

"Thanks for agreeing to talk to me," I

said, sitting next to his desk.

"Coffee?"

"Sure."

He got up to pour me a cup and handed it to me.

"You were on the job, right?"

"That's right."

"The coffee hasn't changed."

I sipped it and said, "Brings back memories."

"Did you make detective?"

"No," I said, "I went out a patrolman."

"Tough break."

I didn't know if he meant never making detective, or the way my career in law enforcement ended.

"Speaking of tough breaks . . ." I said.

"Yeah," Lacy said, "this Mancuso thing. Whew, what a looker. How anyone could kill a woman as fine as that is beyond me."

"You know that Vincent Delvecchio is my brother, right?"

He nodded. "Devlin mentioned it. So, your brother's a priest, huh?"

"That's right," I said. "Father Delvecchio. What have you got on him?"

Lacy sat forward and said, "I'm going to try my best to be helpful here, Mr. Delvecchio, but I hope you understand I can't give you my case." He touched his hair lightly, verifying that it was still in place. "I assume you're going to hire a lawyer for your brother?"

"That's right."

"Well, if your brother is arrested, his lawyer will benefit from his right to disclosure, and he will see all the evidence."

Helpful Detective Lacy sounded more like a lawyer than a cop. I was willing to bet that he was going to law school at night.

"Just between you, me, and the lamppost, Detective," I said, leaning toward him, "how close are you to an actual arrest?"

"We still have some investigating to do, Mr. Delvecchio, before we present our case to the DA. In fact, my partner is out at this very moment, continuing to do preliminaries."

"When will you be getting around to talking to my brother?" He didn't answer right away and I said, "I want to be able to get him a lawyer in time."

"I tell you what," Lacy said. "Get him a lawyer, and have them both come in to see me."

"I think I can arrange that."

"How about Thursday morning?" he suggested. "Ten o'clock?"

I nodded.

"Well, good," Lacy said, standing up

abruptly. He put his hand out and said, "I'm glad we had this little talk, Mr. Delvecchio. I'm always happy to cooperate."

Lacy struck me as the kind of man who never wanted to get anyone mad at him, just in case he ever needed him for something.

But I was thinking, what talk? I hadn't found out a damned thing and he was already giving me the bum's rush — albeit it a very polite one.

I stood up and took his hand, but I didn't let him push me out the door.

"How about throwing me a bone?"

"What do you mean?"

"How'd you get onto my brother?"

He frowned, then gave a little shrug. "Why not? We had a witness who saw him drive up and enter the hotel. It struck us odd, a priest going to a Holiday Inn, *and* he didn't stop at the desk. He went straight up. They got his plate number, and we ran it. Once we knew what church he was, uh, assigned to, we realized it was the victim's parish. It wasn't hard to ID your brother from his description."

"If he had gone there to kill her," I said, "he wouldn't have used a parish car, he wouldn't have worn his collar, and he certainly wouldn't have used the front door."

"True," Lacy said, without missing a beat, "but we're not saying he *went* there to kill her."

Point to him.

"Is it all right with you if I go and look around the motel?"

"The Holiday Inn? Sure, sure." His tone was magnanimous. "It's a public place. The room where she was killed is still sealed, though." The last was said with a warning in his voice, as if he were talking to a small child.

"I don't have to get inside the room," I said. "I just want to snoop around outside."

"Snoop to your heart's content." He waved his right hand in a go-right-ahead gesture, and then while it was out there used it to check his hair again.

I didn't like the man. I had the feeling that he had been laughing at me from the moment I entered the room. No, not laughing . . . *amused* by me.

"Tell me something," I said before leaving, "are you attending law school?"

"Why, yes," he said, smiling. "You really are a detective, aren't you?"

"So I've been told."

12

It was ironic to me that Gloria Mancuso should have picked the Holiday Inn in Staten Island to die in. Just last year I had tailed another faithless wife to the very same hotel. That woman hadn't died as a result of it, but someone had. A cabbie told me that time that when Brooklyn spouses stepped out on their better halves, this Holiday Inn was a popular spot for it. I'd had my doubts then, but I guess he was right.

I drove Hacker's Grand Prix from the precinct to the hotel and parked in their parking lot. I'd forgotten to ask Vinnie how he got to Staten Island. If he had taken one of the Church vehicles, someone might have gotten a license plate. If he had taken a cab, the cabbie could probably ID him. Either way he was fu— um, in trouble.

I went inside and approached the desk clerk. I couldn't remember if he was the one I had spoken to last year. He was wearing the Holiday Inn green jacket and looked to be about college age. He watched me as I approached, appraising me.

"Can I help you?" he asked.

"Yes," I said. "I'm investigating the murder that occurred here Thursday night."

I held my breath, waiting for him to ask me if I was a cop.

"I talked to the other detectives already," he said. "Twice."

"Well, maybe you wouldn't mind going over it again for me, just one more time." I dredged up my cop smile from my past, pasted it on and said, "Please?"

"Look," he said, sighing, "all I saw was the priest come into the lobby. He looked kind of on edge, you know? If he hadn't been a priest, I would have thought he was just some guy meetin' his dolly, you know?"

"What'd he do?"

"He went into the elevator."

"Did you notice what floor he went to?"

"No," the clerk said. "I told the other cops, I didn't see what floor he went to, and I never saw him leave."

"Is there another way he could have gotten out without passing you?"

"If he really wanted to," the clerk said, "there was plenty."

I hadn't asked Vinnie how he left the hotel. There were probably a lot of things I hadn't asked him that I might have asked

84

him if he weren't my brother. Maybe I should keep that in mind next time we talked.

"All right." I took out a five and handed it to him. "Thanks."

I started to walk out, but he called out to me before I reached the door.

"Hey!"

I turned and he beckoned to me. I walked back to the desk.

"The other cops didn't give me nothin'," he said. "Maybe that's why I didn't remember to tell them somethin' else I noticed."

"Like what?"

"Well, the broad, the one who was killed? Man, she was some looker. She had legs that wouldn't quit, and a tight ass —"

"I know all that," I said, cutting him off.

"Yeah, well, there's somethin' you don't know."

"What?"

"She didn't come here alone."

"What?"

"Naw," the kid said, "somebody dropped her off."

"Who?"

"Man, I don't know that. I don't even know what kind of car, only that it was shiny blue."

"What about the doorman who was on duty that night? Would he remember?"

"We don't use a doorman at night all the time," the kid said. "We ain't all that busy, except for . . . well, you know."

"And you didn't have a doorman that night?"

"No."

"How'd you know the car was shiny blue? And how did you know she was dropped off?"

"Well, there ain't much to do here at night, and when a car pulls in you can see the headlights. When I saw the lights I looked out the door. When she opened the passenger door the inside light went on, and I saw her step out. I mean, I saw her legs first. Man, they were —"

"The car."

"Yeah, the light from inside was enough for me to see the color of the car. Shiny blue."

"Did you see the driver?"

"No."

"Man? Woman?"

"Couldn't tell. Hey, I was lookin' at the blonde, ya know?"

"Yeah, right." I took out another five and held it out to him.

"Hey, man, I wasn't hintin' —"

"Forget that," I said. "You earned it."

"Thanks."

I started away, but this time something occurred to me and I turned back.

"One more question."

"Shoot."

"Did she check in?"

"Did she — no, now that you mention it, she went right into the elevator, like she already had a room key. Hey," he said, snapping his fingers, "that means somebody else checked her in, huh?"

"That's what it means," I said. "Listen, can you check something for me?"

"What?"

"I want to know how many keys were given out for that room, and how many you got back. Can you do that for me?"

"I'd have to look it up," he said, "and I can't do it right now."

"That's okay," I said. "If you can do it by tonight, though, I'd appreciate it." I took out another five and gave it to him.

"Where do I call you?"

Now I had to admit I wasn't a cop, because I couldn't have him calling the precinct.

"Look," I said, taking out one of my business cards, "I'm not really a cop . . ."

He took the card and said, "You never

said you were, man. I'll give you a call to-night."

"Thanks. If I'm not in, just leave the in-formation on my machine. When I get it, I'll drop a twenty in the mail to you. Okay?"

"Sure, man," he said enthusiastically.

I noted his name on his jacket — "Riley" — so I could mark the envelope to his atten-tion.

"When did you know I wasn't a cop?" I asked him before leaving.

He grinned and said, "When you laid that first five on me, man."

13

I drove Hacker's car back over the Verrazano Bridge to Brooklyn, dropped it off by his apartment, and took a cab to my place. I could have walked it, but I was in a hurry to get back. I had to line up a lawyer for Vinnie. I knew plenty of lawyers. I had *worked* for plenty of them, but I had to get one that I would trust with my brother's life. My problem was I didn't know one who fit the bill. I did know, however, that Miles Jacoby had a friend who was a lawyer, a man he thought very highly of. His name was Hector Delgado, and he had his office in Manhattan.

I pulled out a Manhattan phone book and looked up his number. I would have preferred to wait for Jack, so that he could introduce us, but I didn't have time. Jack wouldn't be calling in until after five, and Delgado would not have office hours then. Since I had promised that Vinnie and his lawyer would stop in to see Detective Lacy and his partner at 10 A.M. Thursday morning, I had to get Vinnie together with a lawyer as soon as possible.

I dialed Delgado's number and his secretary answered. I asked for Hector Delgado, and she told me that he was in court.

"Listen," I said, "it's very important that I talk to him. My name is Nick Delvecchio; I'm a PI out of Brooklyn."

There was a pause and then she asked, "Are you Miles Jacoby's friend?"

"That's right."

"He's mentioned you," she said. "I'm Missy. I'll have Mr. Delgado call you back as soon as he gets in, Mr. Delvecchio."

"My name is Nick, Missy," I said. "I'm gonna wait right here until he does call me back. Thanks."

"Okay, Nick," she said, her tone friendly, and we hung up.

I remembered Missy. She had worked for Jacoby's mentor, Eddie Waters, before Waters was killed. Jacoby found Waters' killer, and Missy later went to work for Hector Delgado.

I was glad Missy recognized my name. That meant Delgado might, but if he didn't, she'd tell him. I felt fairly confident that I would hear from him today.

Next I called Vinnie at the Rectory, but he wasn't there. I left a message with Sister Olivia for him to call me back.

I checked my watch. It was four o'clock

and I was hungry, but I couldn't leave until I got my calls. I went out into the hall and knocked on Sam's door. I left the door to my office open, so I'd hear the phone if it rang.

Sam answered, and I knew she'd been working. Her hair was tousled, as if she had been running her hands through it between paragraphs, and the tart, pleasant scent of girl sweat made its way to my nostrils. She says that even in an air-conditioned room, when she's writing she sweats. I told her women don't sweat, they glow.

A while back I used to be able to tell if she was working just by listening at her door. That was back when she had a typewriter, and, later, one of those noisy printers. These days, you couldn't hear the printers unless you were in the same room with them.

Sam doesn't look like Sissy Spacek, but she's got the same hair and eyebrows. However, the resemblance stopped there. From the neck down Sam looked more like a playboy centerfold. Right now she was wearing a T-shirt which did nothing to hide the fact that her firm breasts were unfettered.

"Nick, hi."

"You got anything to eat?"

"What?"

"I'm hungry," I said, "and I can't leave the building. I'm waiting for some important calls."

She leaned against the doorjamb and folded her arms beneath her breasts.

"Did you break that answering machine already?"

"No, the machine works fine, it's just that I have to be here to get those messages personally."

"Well, I'm very sorry," she said, "but my cupboard is bare."

"Great," I said. "Why couldn't I get a neighbor who can cook?"

"Sorry, friend," she said wryly, "but you got one with looks."

I suddenly realized what a bore I was being, so I smiled and said, "I sure did. You know, with your build, you shouldn't wear T-shirts. It's too dangerous."

"For who?"

"For the male population of Brooklyn."

"Well," she said, "when I'm working, I like to be comfortable."

"I can see that," I said. "Look, I'm sorry I bothered you. I'll send out for a pizza."

"Get it with pepperoni," she said, raising her eyebrows, "and I'll split it with you."

"You got a deal," I said. "I'll call you when it's here."

"Fine," she said, "and while we're eating it, you can tell me what's the matter with you."

"Does it show?"

She smiled and said, "It does to me, Nicky."

I made a face at her and she closed the door. She knows I hate it when anyone outside my family calls me that.

I went back into my office and called for a pizza from a nearby pizzeria. I ordered it with *half* pepperoni.

14

Over pizza and beer in my kitchen — I always have beer in the fridge — I told Sam what was going on. I even told her about Vinnie. Sam is probably my best friend, and she's as level-headed as they come — or as level-headed as someone who is trying to write for a living can be.

"Your brother is no killer, Nick," she said when I was through.

"I know that."

"And he'd never break his vows."

"I know that, too," I said, then squinted at her suspiciously and asked, "How do *you* know that?"

"I've met your brother."

"Yeah, but . . . you never made a pass at my brother, did you?"

"Well, no . . . but he is real good-looking, you know?"

"I know, I know," I said. "He looks like an actor."

"Or a model."

"So you've got a thing for my brother?" I asked. "Is that it?"

She grinned at me and took a big bite from a slice of pizza. A big glob of cheese slid off and fell onto her chest.

"Serves you right," I said, while she tried to wipe up the mess with a napkin.

"So," she said, "what are you gonna do?"

"I've got to get my brother together with the lawyer, so the lawyer can tell us what to do."

"Why are you rushing this?"

"Lacy was too smug," I said. "I think he wants to arrest my brother."

"On what evidence?"

"He was there," I said, "and I can't have him deny that. Once they arrest him, if he tells them anything about his three meetings with Gloria Mancuso, he's gonna look even more guilty."

"Will he tell them?"

"I guess that'll be up to the lawyer."

"Who's the lawyer?"

"Hector Delgado," I said, "a friend of Miles Jacoby's."

"Jacoby's that PI from the city?"

"Yeah," I said, "the one who's watching Dan Kellogg for me."

"How are you gonna keep working for Linda Kellogg when your own brother needs your help?"

"I don't know," I said. "Maybe I should just drop her case —"

"You can't do that!" Sam said. "Her husband's a brute. She needs somebody to protect —"

"She needs *somebody*," I said, "that's the key word. It doesn't have to be me. Maybe I'll just turn the whole thing over to Jacoby, if he wants it."

"And if he doesn't?"

"There are other PIs who could use the work." I saw a look come into her eyes and she eased forward in her chair.

"What?" I said.

She picked up a napkin and wiped pizza oil from her hands so she could use them when she spoke. If I didn't know better, I would have sworn the girl was Italian.

"Let me do it."

"Sam —"

"No, no," she said, waving her hands, "I can do it. Let me follow him."

"You can't."

"Why not?"

"You're not trained."

"Nick, anybody can follow somebody —"

"Hell no," I said, "you have to be trained for surveillance work —"

"Nick," she said, "I've read so many books —"

"Reading about it and doing it are two different things, Sam."

She stared at me and then said, "What's the real reason you don't want me to do it?"

"The real reason?"

"Yeah."

"Your tits are too big."

"What?"

"There's no way you could follow someone and go unnoticed," I said. "Also, your hair is too blond."

"Am I supposed to take this as a compliment?" she asked. "My hair's too blond, my tits are too big . . . I tell you what. I'll wear a hat and tuck my hair up underneath, and I'll wear a big, floppy sweatshirt." Her hands were gesticulating wildly.

"A floppy sweatshirt?" I asked. "Sam, it's Indian summer." The temperature that day had hit 85 degrees.

"So," she said, wiggling her pale eyebrows at me, "I won't wear anything underneath."

I was having visions of that when the phone rang.

"Hold that thought."

I went into my office to take the call. It was Miles Jacoby.

"He was clean today, Nick," he said. "In

and out. He didn't even go out to lunch."

"Par for the course, Jack."

"You want me to take him again to-morrow?"

I hesitated, then said, "No, I may have that covered. There is something you can do for me, though."

"Name it."

"Well, actually," I said a bit sheepishly, "I've already used your name."

"What are you talking about?"

"Let me explain."

I went on to tell him about the trouble Vinnie was in, and about having called Hector Delgado.

"Heck can do the job for you, Nick," Jack said. "I'll give him a call right now."

"I don't want this to be a favor, Jack," I said. "We'll pay his fee."

Jack laughed and said, "Heck won't have any problem with that, Nick. Let me get off. He might be trying to call you, and I'll try to call him. Talk to you later."

"Thanks, Jack."

I hung up and went back into the apartment. Sam had taken the opportunity to get a piece ahead of me.

"You shouldn't eat so much pizza," I said, sitting down opposite her again.

"Why not?"

I picked up a slice and said, "You're gonna have to be light on your feet when you're tailing Dan Kellogg tomorrow."

15

Sam had gone back to her apartment to work when the phone rang again. This time it was Heck Delgado.

"Mr. Delvecchio?"

"Speaking."

"Hector Delgado here. I understand you wanted to talk to me."

Delgado had a definite Ricardo Montalban accent that probably served him well in court, especially with female jurors.

"Have you spoken to Miles Jacoby yet?"

"Not this evening. Why? Is Miles involved in this?"

"Only to the extent that I called you because of what I've heard about you from him."

"Well, I'm glad Miles has spoken highly of me. Suppose you tell me what the problem is?"

I did, from beginning to end. He asked some relevant questions along the way, but otherwise listened in complete silence. The only thing I left out for the moment was the fact that I had made an appointment for him and Vinnie to be in the 122nd Precinct on Thursday, at 10 A.M.

"Well," he said when I was finished, "this sounds very interesting."

"Does that mean you'll represent my brother?"

"When may I speak with him?"

"As soon as possible. Well, there is something I didn't mention," I said, and told him about the appointment.

"Well, I don't like that," he said, "but perhaps we can work with it. I will have to speak to your brother first, though. May I see him tonight?"

"I'll arrange it."

"Where?"

I took a moment to think. We couldn't go to the Rectory, because we didn't want anyone there to know about this yet. The same was true of my father's house.

"Would a restaurant, or a diner, be okay?"

"I would rather talk somewhere more quiet. I can understand why you wouldn't want me to go to the Rectory at this point. What about your apartment?"

"That's fine with me," I said. "I'll set it up."

"Would 8 P.M. be convenient?"

"Sure."

"Very well," he said, "all I would need now from you is directions. Would you give them to my secretary for me?"

"No problem," I said. "I appreciate this, Mr. Delgado."

"Not at all," he said. "Please hold on."

I held for less than a minute and then Missy came on and took down the directions. She said that Delgado would be driving, so I simply gave him directions from the Brooklyn Bridge on.

I hung up the phone and it rang almost immediately. It was Vinnie.

"Can you get out tonight?"

"Of course," he said, "I'm not a prisoner here, Nick."

"Well, be here by seven-thirty," I said. "I've got a lawyer coming at eight."

"Who is it?"

"His name is Hector Delgado. He was recommended by a friend."

"Can't we do this tomorrow?"

"No," I said, and told him why.

"Nick, you think they're gonna arrest me?"

"Vinnie," I said, "let's talk about it when you get here, okay?"

"All right," he said. "I'll be there soon."

"You remember where it is?"

"I remember."

"Okay, see you soon."

I hung up and went and checked the refrigerator. I had enough beer, so I didn't have to go out. I was wondering if I should make some coffee when there was a knock on the door to my office. I opened it and Sam was standing there.

"I heard your phone, and my curiosity got the better of me."

"Would you like to make some coffee?" I asked quickly.

"Well . . . sure."

"Come on in . . ."

16

Vinnie arrived well before Delgado, which pleased me. We'd have a chance to talk. When Vinnie entered and saw Sam he smiled.

"Miss Karson," he said.

"I thought we settled that last time, Father," she said, kissing him on the cheek. "Call me Sam."

"It's good to see you again, Sam," he said. "That's not my brother's coffee I smell."

"No," she said, smiling, "he was smart enough to ask me to make the coffee."

Not only had she made the coffee, but she had gone out and picked up some doughnuts for us. The only place that was open was the bodega with the sign in the window about drugs. She'd managed to find a box of Hostess doughnuts with a current expiration date. She had set them out nicely on a plate and covered them with a paper towel.

"The coffee is all ready," she said, "and I have to get back to work."

"Must you leave me with him?" Vinnie asked, jerking his thumb at me.

"I'm sorry, Father, but I must."

"I'll walk you to your apartment."

"Just walk me to the door, Nick."

I did that, and opened it for her. I put my arm around her waist and said, "Thanks, Sam."

"Thank you," she said. "I'll pick Dan Kellogg up at home in the morning and stay on him all day."

"Look," I said, squeezing her, "be careful, all right? If he sees you, break it off."

"He won't see me," she said, smiling broadly. "I have the perfect disguise."

"You gonna dye your eyebrows and eyelashes?"

She elbowed me in the ribs and said, "I'll talk to you tomorrow evening."

I watched her enter her apartment, and then closed the door to mine.

"She's prettier than I remembered," my brother said. I almost made a comment about her having the hots for him, but then I remembered why we were there.

"Want a cup of coffee while we wait?" I asked.

"Sure."

We went into the kitchen and sat at the table. Sam had prepared a twelve-cup pot in the coffeemaker, so it wasn't going to hurt for us to have two while we waited for

Delgado to arrive.

"Tell me what happened in Staten Island," Vinnie said.

I laid it out for him, including what I had found out at the Holiday Inn.

"But . . . who could have brought her there?" he asked when I was done.

"I don't know, Vinnie. Do you know what kind of car her family has?"

"No."

"I'll check into that."

"You think her husband took her there? That's crazy, Nick."

"I don't know what to think, Vinnie," I said. "One thing I'm gonna have to do is find out how their marriage was doing."

"I don't know, but if she was happy, would she have approached me?"

"One has nothing to do with the other, brother," I said. "There are plenty of women who are happy with their husbands who still fool around, and vice versa."

"I guess I just don't understand today's morality," Vinnie said, shaking his head.

"Vinnie," I said, "how did you leave the Holiday Inn that night?"

He averted his eyes and said, "I used the side exit."

"Why?"

"I . . . didn't want to be seen."

"But you went in through the front door, and you were seen."

"When I went there, I managed to convince myself that I was doing so for a noble cause. I don't know if I really believed that she intended to kill herself, but I couldn't take the chance."

"And later?"

"Later," he said, looking into his coffee cup, "I was just running. I was ashamed, and I didn't want anyone to see me."

"Vinnie, what did *you* have to be ashamed of?"

"Nick." He looked at me and I could see the anguish in his eyes. "I failed her."

I couldn't believe what I had just heard.
"What?"

"She needed me, and I failed her."

"She needed you, all right, in her bed."

"No, I don't mean that," he said, "I mean she needed me to save her soul."

"You can't save the world, Vinnie."

"This wasn't the world, Nick," he said, "this was one disturbed, misguided woman."

"Vin—" I said, but there was a knock on the door. I looked at my watch. Delgado was fifteen minutes early.

"Vinnie," I said, standing up, "it's important that you talk openly to Delgado. If he's going to represent you, he's gonna

107

have to know everything."

"He's not going to represent me," Vinnie said, "or know anything unless you let him in."

I went to let him in.

17

Heck Delgado looked just the way I expected him to look. He was tall, well-groomed, in excellent shape, maybe a little younger than I had expected. I didn't think he was yet forty, or if he was, he had just made it. Between him and my brother, I felt like the sad sack of the three. I was glad Sam hadn't seen Delgado. He *wasn't* a priest, and I may not have been able to get her to leave.

Delgado and I shook hands at the door. He had a firm handshake. In his left hand he was holding what looked like an alligator-hide attaché case. The watch on his wrist wasn't a Rolex, but it still had to cost a bundle.

"I spoke to Miles before I came," he said. "He has a very high opinion of you."

"I feel the same about him." What else would we say about each other? "My brother is in the kitchen. This way."

"I understand you used to be a police officer."

"That's right," I said, "but not for about five years."

In the kitchen I introduced Vinnie to him as Father Vincent Delvecchio.

"Father, a pleasure," Delgado said.

"Mr. Delgado."

"Coffee?" I asked.

"Yes, that would be nice," Delgado said, sitting at the table.

I brought him a cup of coffee and then uncovered the doughnuts. He opened his attaché case and took out a normal yellow ruled pad. I don't know what I expected to come out of that alligator-hide case. Maybe a pad in gold leaf. He had a silver and a gold Cross pen in his shirt pocket. He chose the silver.

"I haven't had a chance to eat dinner," Delgado said, and took one of the doughnuts. He looked at us and said, "Gentlemen, for the next half hour or so, you are going to talk and I am going to listen. I want to know everything that you can tell me about this case, down to the smallest detail. Father, why don't you start?"

Vinnie told Delgado how he had first met the Mancusos, Anthony and Gloria. It was several years earlier, when they transferred their daughter into the school. At first he only saw them in church, and at church functions. After a year or so Vinnie became involved with the PTA, and Gloria

Mancuso was also active there. A year after that she became president of the PTA, and they worked even more closely together.

"You never noticed an attraction to you?" Delgado asked. He had started on his second doughnut, and I freshened his coffee. He had been taking notes the entire time. He had a rather large, flowing handwriting that I found difficult to read upside down.

"Mr. Delgado," my brother said slowly, "when you are a young priest, there is a tendency for some mothers to . . . to flirt with you."

"Is there a tendency to flirt back?" he asked.

"No," Vinnie said, growing tense.

"Father," Delgado said, putting his Cross pen down carefully on top of the pad. "I am not your enemy. If I agree to represent you, I will want you to consider me your only friend in the world. Please don't take offense at anything I ask you. I have good reasons for all my questions."

"I'm sorry," Vinnie said. "I've thought about this a lot. I never considered myself a . . . a flirt, but I have become . . . more relaxed with some mothers than others. Gloria may have been one of those mothers. But I never intended . . ."

"No, of course you didn't," Delgado said. "Please, continue."

Now we got to the part where Gloria Mancuso had first approached Vinnie about her feelings for him.

"Can I say something here?"

Delgado looked at me and said, "Please."

"I don't think we should consider that the dead woman had . . . feelings for my brother. I don't think we should consider that she was in love with him to any degree. I think this was a woman who saw men as a challenge, and she saw my brother as her greatest challenge."

"Was she loose?" Delgado asked. "In general, I mean. Did she have a reputation for playing around?"

"I have no way of knowing that," Vinnie said.

"Well, we'll have to find out," Delgado said.

I assumed that by "we" Delgado meant him and me. Later, I would find out differently.

"Please," Delgado said, picking up his pen, "continue."

I poured him more coffee, but he did not take another doughnut. I hadn't had any yet, so I took a powdered one. He had eaten two plain ones. There were also some that were chocolate-covered. Vinnie hadn't had any.

Vinnie went on and told Delgado everything he had told me. He didn't leave anything out, even though I knew it was difficult for him to discuss it with a stranger.

"Is that all of it?" Delgado asked after Vinnie had stopped talking.

"That's it," Vinnie said. "She was alive when I left her."

"Did you see anyone at the hotel that you knew?"

"No."

"Did you see any vehicles you might have recognized in the parking lot?"

"No."

"You drove there in a car owned by the Church?"

"Yes."

Delgado turned his attention to me.

"I assume you've spoken to the police?"

"Yes."

"Please," he said, "tell me everything you've been told, or learned on your own."

I relayed everything to him that I had learned from Devlin and O'Neal at the six-nine, and from Lacy at the one-two-two. I then told him everything I had found out from the desk clerk.

"Has he called yet about the keys?" he

asked, writing furiously on his pad.

"Not yet."

"I'll want to know what he says as soon as you learn it," he said, "and as soon as you find out anything about that blue car. I will leave you my home phone."

"You'll represent me?" Vinnie asked.

"Yes," Delgado said, "if you want me to."

"Yes," Vinnie said, "yes, I do." I could see that Vinnie was impressed with Delgado's thoroughness.

"Good," Delgado said, capping his pen and sliding it into his pocket. "What is the protocol for this, as regards the Church?"

"Uh, well," Vinnie said, "I'm not altogether sure. We'll have to go to the office of the Diocese, here in downtown Brooklyn. It's on Joraleman Street. Nick said he would go with me."

"You and I will go to the Diocese together," Delgado said. "There is no need for your brother to go."

I almost objected, but decided not to.

"I'll start checking on Gloria Mancuso's marriage," I said.

Delgado looked at me and said, "You've done a fine job up until now, Nick, but I have my own investigators. I'm sure you understand."

I did, but I didn't like it. I opened my

mouth to protest, but Vinnie got there before me.

"Mr. Delgado, I want Nick to work on this."

"Father," Delgado said, "I can appreciate how you feel, but —"

"Mr. Delgado," Vinnie said, cutting the man off, "there's no way I can know for sure whether or not you, or any of your investigators, will believe that I did not kill Gloria Mancuso. I do know, however, that my brother believes me. I need that."

"Father —"

"Also," Vinnie continued quickly, "no one will work as hard for me as my brother will, no matter how much you pay them. He's my brother."

Good for you, brother, I thought, and watched Delgado. After a moment, Delgado smiled at both of us.

"I can't argue with that," he said.

Vinnie extended his hand and Delgado took it.

"Thank you," my brother said.

Delgado looked at me and said, "May I have another cup of coffee? We still have some talking to do."

18

Delgado left before Vinnie.

He shook hands with both of us. He and Vinnie were going to meet downtown in the morning and go to the Diocese together. Meanwhile, he had mapped out a strategy for me to follow, which would put us ahead of the game in the event they arrested Father Vinnie over the weekend.

"We're meeting with the police Thursday morning," he'd said. "There is a chance that they will arrest you right there and then, but I doubt it. If it comes, it will probably come after the weekend. Still, we must be prepared for anything."

We agreed that Heck — he had asked us both to call him that — would call me after he and Vinnie had spoken to the Diocese.

After Heck left, Vinnie came back into the kitchen with me.

"More coffee?" I asked him.

"No."

He sat down and toyed with a doughnut.

"How about a glass of milk?" I asked.

"Sure."

I gave him a glass of milk and sat opposite him. He sipped the milk and gnawed at a chocolate-covered doughnut.

"What do you think?" I asked.

"I like him," Vinnie said. "He impressed me. I think I can have confidence in him."

"Good."

He looked at me and said, "I'm scared, Nick."

"You wouldn't be human if you weren't, Vinnie," I said, "and priest or no priest, you are human, you know."

"I know," he said, "but once we go to the Diocese tomorrow, I may not be a priest for very much longer."

"Don't you expect the Church to stand behind you on this?"

"Yes," he said, "of course." He sounded less than convinced.

"Nick, they can't . . . fire you for getting arrested . . . can they?"

He started shaking his head and then said, "I don't know what they'll do, Nick. I just don't know. I mean, we know that I didn't kill her, but they're also going to be concerned with why I went there that night. There's been a lot in the media lately about fallen priests, you know? The whole Covenant House thing, and that fiasco down south with that woman who slept not only with a priest, but a bishop. God," he said, covering his eyes, "the press will have a field day with this, especially since it's the New York press."

"So," I said, "you might be in a no-win situation."

"I know . . ."

"But that doesn't mean you're not gonna fight . . . right?"

"Fight for what?" he said. "If I'm not a priest, what will I be?"

I looked at him and said, "You'll be out of jail, free, and alive . . . by the grace of God."

He looked at me sharply. I knew why. The last line of my statement surprised even myself.

"Yes," he said, seeming oddly calm suddenly, "by the grace of God."

After Father Vinnie left to go back to the Rectory I rinsed off whatever glasses and dishes had to be rinsed off, then decided to have a beer. I still had two bottles of Dos Equis and two St. Pauli Girls among the Meister Bräus in my refrigerator from the last time I had the money to buy imported beer. I chose Mexican over German and took a Dos Equis into the living room with me so I could go over the day.

First, I wasn't sure I had done the right

thing in letting Sam tail Dan Kellogg the next day. She wasn't a pro, but then neither was Kellogg, so where was the real danger? What were the chances that he'd notice her, especially now, when she would be the third person to tail him in three days? Even if he looked behind him, he wouldn't see the same person. On the other hand, he hadn't looked behind him the entire time I was tailing him. Well, maybe I'd let her tail him one day, and then I could get somebody else.

Wait a minute! I don't know why I didn't think of it before. I knew another Brooklyn PI who, coincidentally, lived in Greenpoint, and owned a bar there. And for good measure, he was Italian. Right, so in the morning I'd call Sal Carlucci and line him up for the next day, and as many days after that, that he could handle. Carlucci was in his fifties, sort of semi-retired, and he had a gimpy leg from when he was a cop, but I was sure he could handle this.

If need be, I could probably rotate Jacoby, Carlucci, and Sam. That way I would be taking up a minimum of their time and still be covering Kellogg full-time.

I looked at my watch. It was too late to call Linda Kellogg at the hospital. I'd call her in the morning, and assure her that I was still on the job.

The Kellogg matter handled, I settled down to think about my brother's problem.

Tomorrow, while he and Heck went to the Diocese, I was going to have to start checking up on Gloria Mancuso. According to Heck, if Vinnie was arrested and went as far as going to trial, all we had to do was raise some reasonable doubt, and finding a passel of boyfriends would certainly do that. Vinnie told me that I could pick up a list of the PTA people in the morning from Sister Olivia, and I could start with them. Once again, as I had done at the Holiday Inn, I'd simply present myself as "investigating" Gloria Mancuso's murder, and let the people assume that I was a cop. In the event they asked for ID, I'd give it to them, and then try to get them to talk to me anyway.

Under normal circumstances, I wouldn't have gone anywhere near an active homicide investigation. That was the fastest way to get my license lifted. This was different, however. This was my brother.

Something that Vinnie and I hadn't yet talked about was how and when we were going to tell Pop and Maria that he was in this jam. It would have to come straight from Vinnie, and he should probably tell both of them at the same time, simply so he wouldn't have to go through it twice.

When we talked tomorrow, I'd broach that subject with him. We could probably wait until we knew whether or not he was going to be arrested. My feeling — and Heck agreed — was that if and when they decided to arrest him, in light of the cooperation we were giving them, they'd probably just call Heck and ask him to have his client give himself up.

Jesus, I thought, how would Vinnie react to being in jail? I squeezed the bottle in my hand and hoped that Father Vinnie's faith in God was strong enough to see him through this.

19

I got to the Rectory nice and early, but still after school started. Sister Olivia answered the door again and smiled at me. I was struck once again at how pretty she was.

"Hello, Mr. Delvecchio," she said, "come in."

"Thank you, Sister."

I entered the foyer and she closed the door behind us.

"This way, please."

I followed her to a small office off to the side. The Rectory smelled just like the Rectory I knew when I was a kid.

"Father left just a little while ago," she said, "but he asked me to give you this."

She handed me an 8½-by-11 sheet of paper. It was a Xerox of a list of the parents in the PTA. Next to their names was their position. Right at the top of the list it said "Gloria Mancuso, President."

"Thank you, Sister."

"Are you, uh, investigating our PTA?" she asked. Before I could answer she said, "Forgive me, but I'm very curious. I, uh, read mysteries, and books about private eyes are my favorites."

"Not Greeley, or Kemelman?"

"No," she said, smiling, "Jeremiah Healy and Sue Grafton."

I tried a shot in the dark.

"Bill Pronzini?"

"Oh, yes," she said, "ever since I was . . . younger."

I was running into a lot of people lately who read mysteries, including my own brother.

"Well, Sister," I said, lowering my voice dramatically, "I really am not at liberty to say, right now."

"Oh," she said, lowering her voice, "client confidentiality, right?"

"That's right." We were staring at each other and I couldn't stop myself, so I asked her, "How could somebody so pretty become a nun?"

She flushed and was about to answer when a distinguished white-haired man walked in, and we both straightened up as if we had been doing something we should feel guilty about.

"Monsignor!" she said.

"Sister," the man said, nodding to me, "have you seen Father Delvecchio?"

"He, uh, left a little while ago, Monsignor."

"Left? To go where?"

"I don't know, Monsignor."

"He didn't say?"

"No, sir," Sister Olivia said. I was edging toward the door when she added, "but this is Father Delvecchio's brother. Perhaps he can help you."

Monsignor Genovese looked at me and raised his white eyebrows. He had a ruddy complexion and light-blue eyes. He would charm the pants — well, he'd charm all the older ladies in the parish.

Weren't there any ugly priests or nuns these days?

"Father Delvecchio's brother?" he said. "How nice." He extended his hand and I shook it.

"Nick Delvecchio, Monsignor. It's a pleasure to meet you. I have to be going —"

"Would you know where your brother went this morning, Mr. Delvecchio?"

"Uh, well . . ." My Catholic background somehow kept me from lying immediately, but I finally got it out. "No, sir, I don't. I really have to go —"

"Would you be able to come into my office with me for a few moments, Mr. Delvecchio?" he asked then. "There's something I want to talk to you about."

"In your office?"

"Just for a few minutes, please."

"Well . . . sure . . ."

"This way, please."

Monsignor left the small office, and I looked at Sister Olivia, who looked distressed. I smiled so she wouldn't feel bad about giving away my identity, and then followed the monsignor.

The monsignor's office was impressive. It was almost big enough to hold the oakwood desk he moved around to sit behind.

"Take a seat, please."

"Monsignor —"

"Please sit!"

I felt like an altar boy again. I sat.

"Mr. Delvecchio, I would like to know what is going on."

"Monsignor?"

"Please," he said, holding his hands up to me, palms out, "don't lie. You did it badly before. You hesitated. I would think that a private investigator would know how to lie better."

"I do," I said, "it's this place."

"Were you ever an altar boy?"

"Yes."

"When was the last time you were in church?"

"Um —"

"Or to confession?"

"Uh —"

"What is going on, Mr. Delvecchio? I know it has something to do with the police taking your brother out of confession on Saturday. It must also have something to do with the death of one of our parishioners, Mrs. Mancuso, eh? Now, if I put two and two together, I *will* come up with four, but perhaps you would like to save me the effort?"

I stared at him for a few moments, and then decided that I couldn't tell him anything, Catholic guilt or not.

"I'm sorry, Monsignor, there's nothing I can tell you. I think you should wait for Vinnie — that is, Father Delvecchio, to return, and then talk to him about it."

He was frowning mightily as I spoke.

"Mr. Delvecchio," he said, "I am not a happy man."

"I understand that, sir."

"Is Vincent in trouble?"

"Again, Monsignor, that's going to be up to him to tell you. I hope you can understand that."

"Your brother had better have a good explanation for me when he returns."

"I think he will, sir," I said. "I also think he's going to need some understanding from you."

"Mr. Delvecchio — Nick," the monsignor said, folding his hands on his desk, "I am a very understanding man, but my understanding, and my patience, both have limits."

"I understand, sir."

He stared at me for a few moments, then nodded and said, "You may go."

"Thank you, sir."

I stopped by Sister Olivia on my way out. She had her legs curled under the chair she was sitting on, and I noticed that she had nice calves. Firm, strong runner's calves.

"Marathoner?" I asked.

"What?" she asked, looking up in surprise.

"I said, are you a marathoner?"

She smiled and said, "I run, but the most I've done is half marathons. How did you know?"

"I, uh . . ." I hesitated, then said, "I noticed your, uh, legs."

She looked down at her legs, then blushed and said, "Oh."

"Do you ever wear your habit?"

"For formal functions," she said, then smiled again and added, "but never when I run."

I opened my mouth to say something, and

then shut it. I realized what I was doing. I was flirting with a nun. Sure, she was a young, attractive female . . . with nice legs . . . but she was still a nun.

"Sister, what can you tell me about Gloria Mancuso?"

The smile, and good-natured expression, left her face at the mention of the dead woman.

"Mr. Delvecchio —"

"Please call me Nick."

"Nick . . . you're asking me an impossible question," she said. "I really can't speak ill of the dead."

"I take it then that you didn't think highly of her."

She compressed her lips for a moment, then looked around.

"She was fine with the children, Nick," she said, "which is why she was a good PTA president."

"She wasn't so good with the adults?"

Sister Olivia stared at me.

"Oh, I think I see," I said. "She got along better with the fathers than the mothers?"

"She was well liked," Sister Olivia said, "by both . . . but for different reasons."

"Sister," I said, touching her arm, "I understand what you're saying."

"Please," she said, "the monsignor —"

"Don't worry, Sister." I was still touching her, so I removed my hand. "I won't say anything to the monsignor."

"Mr. Delvecchio — Nick . . . is Father Vincent in trouble?"

"He might be, Sister," I said, "he might be. In any event, we both appreciate your help."

"If I can really be of any help, please let me know."

"I sure will, Sister."

She got up and walked me to the front door. I started out the door when she opened it, then stopped.

"Sister, excuse me for asking, but . . . have you taken your final vows yet?"

"Oh, yes," she said, "two years ago."

"I see."

"Why?"

"Never mind," I said, shaking my head. "I was just curious."

20

The list Sister Olivia had given me had names, addresses, and phone numbers of all the officers of the PTA. All I could do was go and see the people, and see if they would talk to me.

Given what Sister Olivia had indicated to me about Gloria Mancuso, I thought I'd be getting different reactions from the women than from the men. As early as it was, I'd probably only be finding some of the wives home, and most of the husbands would be at work. There would probably be exceptions, but I prepared a story that I could use on the ladies. After all, most of the PTA positions were held by mothers.

I spent most of the day doing interviews with PTA members and got a variety of responses from them.

The vice president of the PTA was Harriet Dean who, I assumed, would now move up into the presidency. Did that give her a motive? People have been killed for less, but it seemed pretty far-fetched.

Harriet Dean was in her thirties, trying

hard to look younger. She wore tons of makeup that gave her face a brittle look, and tight clothes that bulged in all the wrong places.

What did she think of Gloria Mancuso?

"Gloria was a go-getter," Mrs. Dean said, "and what she usually went and got was men."

"Did her husband know about this?" I asked.

"Well," Mrs. Dean said, "if we did, I assume he did, also."

"What do you mean when you say 'we' did?"

She batted her mascara-laden eyes at me and said, "Why, everyone."

"Well, how did he feel about it?"

"To tell you the truth," she said, "I don't think he cared all that much."

"Why not?"

"Well, he was a busy man. He had other things on his mind," she said, and then used her forefinger to bend her little nose over and added, "if you know what I mean?"

To some people, all Italians are Mafia.

Georgia Taylor was the PTA treasurer. She was younger than both Gloria Mancuso and Harriet Dean, probably just in her mid-twenties.

"I've only been in the PTA a year," she said. "I got the treasurer's job because I was willing to give my time, and because Gloria pushed for me to get it."

"Pushed?"

"She . . . what's the word . . . politicked for me. I really appreciated her help."

"Some of the other women have indicated to me that Gloria may not have been the most faithful wife in the world."

"Did you show me your badge?"

The head of the Hospitality Committee was a very attractive, well-dressed woman in her early thirties named Beverly Smith, whom I caught on her way out. Mrs. Smith struck me as something of a snob.

"I really don't have time to talk with you, officer," she said.

"But I was only after a few words from you about Gloria Mancuso's death."

"I'll give you a few words," she said, pausing as she opened the door of her beemer, "it couldn't have happened to a nicer bitch."

After a while the names and titles ran together. There was a group of women who spoke quite cattily about Gloria, painting her as a hard worker, but also a hard player.

They didn't approve of her attitude toward their husbands. This group was definitely not made up of her friends.

"Was this attitude only directed toward the husbands?" I asked one lady.

"Mister," one young, sweet-faced, very Catholic-looking mother named Molly McBain said, "she tried to fuck anything with a zipper. I wouldn't be surprised if she nailed a priest in the confessional. That would be the kind of challenge Gloria would have liked."

"Any particular priest?"

"Well, the best-looking one was Father Delvecchio," she said, "but as long as he had a zipper, he was fair game. I told all of this to the other police detectives."

"I'm just backtracking a bit . . ." I said.

I wondered which detective she had told that to, and if she had mentioned Vinnie's name.

The other group, her friends — including Harriet Dean and Georgia Taylor — seemed to have put her up on a pedestal, all of them thrilled with her alleged sexual exploits. None of them, however, could come up with any names for the men she had on a string. All of them, quite obviously, got their kicks vicariously through her and her stories.

I asked one woman, "Do you mean she bragged about having other men?"

"Darling," the woman told me, "what's the point of having them if you can't brag about them?"

I found several husbands home. Since many mothers worked these days, it made sense I'd find some men home. It only took one of the men to sum up their opinion of Gloria Mancuso, though.

"She was a cock tease," the man said, with a four-year-old clinging to his leg, "but what a looker, man."

"Did she ever come across?"

"Well, man," the fella said, "I don't exactly kiss and tell, you know?"

Especially when you've got nothing to kiss and tell about, I thought.

By 5 P.M. I was talked out, and I had a pretty good picture of Gloria Mancuso. She was a hard worker for the PTA, and for the kids, but she didn't let that stop her from having her fun. She was certainly a flirt and a tease, and she had friend and foe alike convinced that she slept around, but no one could give me any specific names. Only one man's name had been mentioned, and that was Vinnie's, but the person who mentioned it certainly didn't know anything definite.

Still, if she had mentioned his name to a detective, it could be very damaging — especially if that detective lacked imagination.

Having spoken to three of the four detective who were involved with the case so far, I thought that was pretty likely.

21

I took a cab home and got there by six-thirty. There was one message on the machine. It was from Sam. She just wanted to tell me that it was 3 P.M. and everything had gone all right so far. She said she'd talk to me tonight. She sounded both pleased and excited.

I made a quick call to Sal Carlucci in Greenpoint. He said he couldn't help me tomorrow and was tied up on the weekend, but he'd be free on Monday, if I still needed him. I told him I'd let him know by Sunday.

I was disappointed not to find a message from Vinnie. I had thought about stopping by the Rectory on my way home, but I didn't want to run into Monsignor Genovese again. I was also a little ashamed of the way I'd flirted with Sister Olivia. Her manner could be called flirtatious, although I was sure she didn't mean it to be, and I wondered if that was the kind of thing Vinnie had meant when he mentioned that he was more "relaxed" with some mothers than with others. I was sure that Sister Olivia had flirted back quite innocently, not meaning anything by it.

Was that how it had started with Gloria and Vinnie? And had it led to disaster?

I went across the hall and knocked on Sam's door. When she didn't answer I started to worry. Kellogg usually made it home by six or so and by routine, stayed there. Sam should have been at home by now. I decided to give her half an hour more before I really started to worry.

As soon as I reentered my apartment, the phone started to ring. I went into the office and picked it up on the third ring. The machine answers on the fourth.

"Delvecchio," I said.

"Nick, this is Heck."

"Heck, how'd it go?"

"We spent quite a bit of time at the Diocese office. As it turned out, we talked with some of their legal advisers. I managed to convince them that I did not need a Father Shannon as an assistant on this."

"Father Shannon?"

"Apparently the Church sent Father Shannon to law school, and he *is* a lawyer, but I doubt that he's ever been involved in anything like this."

"How did they react?"

"At first they were shocked and dismayed. That quickly degenerated into worry and panic. I only wish I could say they were worried about your brother."

"What *were* they worried about?"

"The image of the Church," Heck said. "Did I tell you that I am a lapsed Catholic?"

"Is that different than being a non-practicing Catholic, like me?"

"Yes," Heck said, "if you call yourself a non-practicing Catholic, that means that you either admit that there is a chance you'll go back, or you have a brother who is a priest."

"One out of two."

"With me, there is no chance I could go back. The reasons are very personal and go back many years, but seeing their reaction to Father Vincent's predicament, I am even more convinced that I made the right decision."

"Heck," I said with concern, "are they gonna back Vinnie on this?"

There was a long silence, and then he said, "They said they will."

"You don't believe them?"

"Like anyone else," Heck said, "what the Catholic Church says and does can be two different things."

"What happens now?"

"With the Church? They want Vincent to go to Manhattan."

"To see the cardinal?"

"We will find out who he is to see when we get there."

"When will that be?"

"Friday."

"Are you still on for the one-two-two tomorrow?"

"We will be there," he said. "How did your day go?"

"Well, in the morning I was called in by Vinnie's monsignor. He's no dope," I said, and filled him in on our conversation.

"Your brother will have to handle that this evening," Heck said. "He probably only just got back to the Rectory a little while ago. What else happened? What did you get on Gloria Mancuso?"

"What I figured to get," I said, "not that it helps us a lot. A lot of heresy and rumors." I told him what the other mothers and fathers thought of Gloria, and he took it all in in silence.

When I was finished there were a few moments of silence. I assumed he was taking notes. After a few moments he spoke.

"What you need . . . to do . . ." he said, and he spoke as if he were still writing, speaking with divided attention, ". . . is find her best friend."

"Well, I certainly didn't do that today. It's

possible that whoever it is is not involved in the PTA."

"Yes, of course," he said, "by all means go outside the PTA. Is there someone there who might be able to help you with that?"

"Yes," I said, thinking of Sister Olivia, "there might be."

"Good, good," he said. "All right. We'll speak again tomorrow, after your brother and I talk to the detectives assigned to the case."

"All right, Heck," I said. "Thanks for calling."

I hung up and thought about Sister Olivia again. She probably wouldn't want to talk to me in the Rectory, where the monsignor might see us.

I wondered if nuns accepted invitations to lunch.

22

I kept the door to my apartment open until I heard Sam coming down the hall. I looked at my watch and saw that it was after nine. I catapulted off the sofa and ran to the door as she was putting her key in the lock.

"Where the hell have you been?" I demanded.

She jumped at least a foot and placed her hand over her heart.

"Jesus, you scared the shit out of me!"

"And you scared the shit out of me," I countered. "And what are you doing dressed like that?"

She was wearing a black dress so tight it was hard to imagine how she had gotten it on. It covered her to her neck, but she still looked naked because her breasts were plainly and perfectly outlined. You could even see her nipples. It also had no sleeves and shoulders, and her pale skin stood out starkly against the black. At the other end it was so short that I could see the tops of her net black stockings. On her feet she was wearing black boots with high heels. Her usually pale eyelashes were covered with dark mascara, and she was wearing more makeup than I had ever seen her wear.

"That's your idea of going unnoticed when you're tailing someone?" I demanded.

"Look, Nick, let me change and then I'll explain."

"The hell with changing," I said, grabbing her arm, "explain now, dammit!"

"Don't yell at me," she said, pulling on her arm to get it away from me, but I wasn't letting go. I pulled her right into my apartment and shut the door, *then* I let her go.

"Friends don't yell at each other," she told me belligerently.

"No, but employers yell at employees, and you were supposed to be working for me today, not going out on a date."

"I *was* working for you today. If you'll shut up long enough, I'll tell you about it."

"All right," I said, folding my arms across my chest, "talk."

"I picked Kellogg up at his home this morning and followed him to work."

"Dressed like that?"

"No, I wasn't dressed like this," she shot back. "Are you gonna let me tell it?"

"Tell it," I said tightly.

"I stayed with him, but he never even left

his place for lunch. After work he didn't go straight home."

"What?" I unfolded my arms. "That's a break in pattern."

"I know."

"Where'd he go?"

"Aldretti's."

Aldretti's was only a few blocks from our building.

"What was he doing there?"

"Well, I looked in the window and he sat in a booth, not at the bar. If he had sat at the bar I might have figured he was there for a quick drink, but since he took a booth I thought he'd be there awhile. That's when I got the idea."

"What idea?"

"I ran home and got out my fuck-me dress," she said, doing a slow pirouette. Jesus, I could see the cleft between her buttocks.

"Sam —"

"Nick," she said, "we wanted to find out if he was a chaser, right? What better way than to dangle some bait in front of him?"

"I didn't send you out there to be bait!"

"I know, I know, but I decided to use some initiative. Isn't that what a good detective does?"

"I guess I wouldn't know," I said. "Go

on. What happened when you got back to the bar?"

Suddenly her face fell.

"I don't think he ever looked at me."

"Well, that makes him either blind, dead, or . . . gay."

"If he was gay, there are other places for him to go than Aldretti's."

"Okay, so if he didn't come on to you, what did he do?"

"He met a guy."

"A guy?"

"He must have been waiting for him, because the guy came in and sat right down with him. He didn't even have to look for him, just walked right to the booth."

"What happened then?"

"They argued. I couldn't hear what they were saying because I was sitting at the bar, too far away, and I was fending off every other guy in the bar."

"You don't frequent Aldretti's, do you?"

"I don't hang out in bars, Nick," she said. "At least, not bars like Aldretti's."

"My point is, no one there knew you."

"No," she said, "but they all wanted to."

"I can't say I blame them."

"What?"

"What else happened?"

"Nothing. They had a beer each, argued

for a while, and then Kellogg calmed down and the other man talked to him for a long time."

"Did Kellogg look like he might be afraid of this other guy?"

"I don't see why he would be," she said. "The other guy was a lot smaller, a real skinny, frail-looking guy."

"Fear doesn't have to be something physical, Sam. Maybe the guy's got something on Kellogg."

"What?"

"I don't know."

"You think he's got a past he doesn't want anyone to know about?"

"Could be. I'll have to have it checked out."

"I could do it."

"You?" I said in disbelief.

"Why not?"

"Sam, you are not a detective, and you proved that today."

"I thought I did pretty well today."

"You did, until you got this crazy idea to dress up. Look at you."

She looked down at herself, then at me.

"What's the matter with the way I look?"

"Well, it's a little cheap, isn't it?"

"Cheap?"

"Sam, you look dangerous," I said.

"Walking around like that you could start fights, cause traffic accidents."

She peered at me suspiciously and said, "Are you complimenting me?"

"I'm scolding you, dammit!" I said. "Don't you know when you're being yelled at?"

"For what? I found out he wasn't interested in other women."

"You found out that he wasn't interested in *you*," I said, "not today, anyway. You also drew a lot of attention to yourself, when you were supposed to be running surveillance *without* drawing attention. Whether you think so or not, he must have seen you, which means I can't use you anymore."

"But —"

"No buts," I said. "I have someone lined up to take him on Monday."

"What about Thursday and Friday? And the weekend? If he's got a girlfriend, won't he try to see her on the weekend?"

"I don't think he's got a girlfriend," I said. "I think there's something else making him so mad."

"What?"

"I don't know," I said, "and I don't have the time to try and find out myself. I'm going to have to go and see Linda and tell her that I'm turning the case over to someone else."

"Who?"

"Whoever wants it. Jacoby, Carlucci, Henry Po. If they don't want it, maybe they can recommend someone who will."

"Linda Kellogg is counting on you, Nick."

I rubbed my hand over my face and said, "I know, but so is my brother."

23

"What's happening with your brother?" Sam asked.

"Let's finish this up first," I said, "and then I'll tell you."

"There's nothing to finish up. He left Aldretti's and I followed him home."

"Wait a minute," I said, slowing her down. "Who left first, him or the other guy?"

"He did."

"Did the other guy see you?"

"I . . . think so. He looked over at the bar a couple of times. He could have been looking at me."

"Bet on it. I don't want you going near Aldretti's anymore."

"I told you," she said, "I don't hang out at neighborhood bars . . . although there were a couple of good-looking guys with interesting offers. You know what one of them wanted to do with whipped cream?"

"I don't want to know," I said quickly. "You're off the case, Karson, and you've got a book to write."

"Oh, shit," she said. "I forgot about that."

"Better get to work."

"What about Linda Kellogg?"

"She's safe in the hospital, Sam," I said. "Go on, go back to work."

"First tell me what happened with your brother."

I gave her the short version, telling her that we really wouldn't know much until after he and Heck Delgado had met with the detectives.

"Well, keep me informed, all right?"

"Sure."

"What about your family?"

"They don't know yet."

"Are you going to tell them?"

"I think Vinnie should do that."

"You're probably right."

She headed for the door, opened it, and then turned and said, "What do you really think of this dress?"

I took a moment to look at her. Sam's not really tall, but I think she'd qualify as a big, healthy woman. She looked fabulous in the dress, especially with her shoulders and arms showing. Sam works out, and you can tell she does from the wonderful muscle tone in her arms and shoulders. She lifts weights, and has said on occasion that she might have done so seriously if her tits weren't too big.

Her pale skin and blond hair really played well off the black dress. I had that rare thought about why we were just friends — good friends, granted, but why just friends?

"Sam," I said, "you don't need a fuck-me dress to attract attention."

It was the only harmless thing I could think of saying. I couldn't tell her that seeing her dressed that way, with her nipples so plainly pressing against the material of the dress, made my heart rise up into my throat. That's not the kind of thing one friend says to another.

She thought about that for a moment, and said, "I think I'll take that as a compliment."

"It was meant that way."

"Now tell me why you were so mad at me."

"That's easy," I said. "I was worried about you."

"Really?"

"Really."

She walked back to me and kissed me on the cheek. I could smell the fresh scent of her hair. I loved the way her hair smelled.

"You're sweet," she said. "Thanks for giving me the chance."

"You're welcome," I said, and as she walked back to the door I said, "As a detective, you weren't exactly a total fuck-up."

"Now that," she said, with the doorknob in her hand, "I *will* take as a compliment."

Once she was out of the apartment and out of my sight in that dress, I sat down and waited for my breathing to return to normal.

I was thinking about Riley, the clerk at the Holiday Inn, when the phone rang. He was supposed to call me back about the room keys, and I was hoping this was he.

I couldn't have been more wrong.

"Nicholas?"

There was only one man I knew who called me Nicholas.

"Hello . . ." When speaking to Dominick Barracondi, I always had a problem with what to call him. Nicky "Barracuda" had been a friend of my father's for years, even before he rose to be the Godfather of Brooklyn. My problem was that he was also *my* godfather, and I could never bring myself to call him that. It always summoned up visions of Marlon Brando with his mouth stuffed with cotton.

I didn't approve of my godfather, but I always treated him with respect.

"How are you?" he asked.

"Just fine."

"And your father?"

"He's fine, too."

"Please give Vito my best, and your lovely sister, too."

"I will, sir."

"Nicholas, I was wondering if you would come and see me tomorrow."

"About what?"

"I . . . would prefer to discuss that when you are here — if you would be kind enough to come?"

That was the closest I'd ever heard Nicky Barracuda come to saying "please."

I frowned, wondering what he wanted.

"Well . . . all right." Curiosity kept me from saying no.

"Come for lunch?"

"Yes."

"Excellent! It has been some time since we have talked."

"Is that all you want to do," I asked, "talk? Pass the time?"

"Uh, no, no, I have something very specific in mind. I will see you at one, eh?"

"One is fine."

"Good, good. See you then, Nicholas."

I hung up, puzzled, and then a dim light dawned. He had asked about everyone in my family except Vinnie. He always asked about "Father Vinnie." Why not this time? Did he know Vinnie was in trouble? Was that what he wanted to see me about?

If he did know, how?

The answer was simple.

He was, after all, Nicky "Barracuda."

24

At about eight the next morning I was at the Rectory again. And once again I was driving Hacker's Grand Prix. I had called ahead to make sure Vinnie would be there to see me. I knew that he'd be leaving for Staten Island at about eight-fifteen, to meet Heck at the one-two-two.

A woman who wasn't Sister Olivia answered the door. She was a hard-looking forty-five, squat and gray-haired, wearing wire-rimmed glasses.

"Good morning, Sister."

"I'm not a nun," she said. "My name is Mrs. Graf. I'm staff. Can I help you?"

"I'm sorry," he said. "Without the habit it's hard to tell."

If she sympathized with my predicament, it didn't show on her face.

"My name is Nick Delvecchio," I said. "Father Delvecchio is my brother. I'd like to see him, please."

"Step in and wait, please."

I stepped inside. She closed the door and went off into the bowels of the Rectory.

While I was waiting in a sort of waiting room, the monsignor came by.

"Good morning, Monsignor."

"I don't know if I should speak to you, Mr. Delvecchio," the monsignor said.

"Monsignor —"

"I am certainly more angry at Father Delvecchio for not having enough faith in me to confide in me before he went to the Diocese," he said, "but I have enough anger left over for you, too."

"I hope you have enough forgiveness for both of us, Monsignor."

The older man pointed his forefinger at me and said, "Don't patronize me, young man."

"I'm not, Monsignor," I said. "I'm serious, more for my brother than for me. He was unsure of what to do and came to me for help. I know you can understand that."

"Of course," he said reluctantly. "You *are* his brother."

"Yes, sir, I am," I said, "and once he did come to me, he had to do what I told him to do. It was I who told him not to tell anyone until after we spoke with a lawyer. My father and sister don't even know about this yet."

"I suspect your father might be even angrier than I am." He started out of the room, then turned at the door and said, "Maybe."

His footsteps had just echoed out when I heard those of Mrs. Graf returning.

"Father will be right down," she said, sticking her head in the door.

"Thank you."

Five minutes later my brother appeared.

"Come on," he said, "walk me out."

Outside, I asked, "How are you?"

"Okay."

"No," I said, "really, Vinnie."

He took a deep, shuddering breath and said, "Right now I'm more nervous than scared. I'll know better later on today."

I walked with him toward the parking lot, which was on East Ninety-eighth Street.

"But you know something?" he said as we walked. "I feel better, somehow. Dealing with it, and dealing with it effectively, has made me feel better, and I have you to thank. Heck, too, but mostly you."

I didn't know how to react to that, so I just put my hand on his shoulder for a moment.

"How was it with the monsignor?"

"He was a little disappointed, and hurt, that I hadn't come to him. He covered it up with anger."

"I know, I got some of that."

"He said he's behind me, though. He knows I'd never break my vows. He also knows what Gloria Mancuso was like."

"Vinnie," I said after a pause, "maybe we should go and see Pop tonight?"

He thought about it for a moment, then said, "Yes, I think so. Will you call him, and Maria, for me?"

"Sure."

We reached the parking lot and stood next to the late-model Ford that he'd be driving.

"Before you go," I said, "uh, you haven't spoken to Dominick about this, have you?"

"Dominick?"

We both knew whom I was talking about. In my family, Nicky Barracuda had always been "Dominick." For a while he was even "Uncle Dominick," but that changed as we got older. Even in my own mind I referred to him now as Barracondi.

"Why would I do that?"

"I was just wondering."

"You wouldn't ask me that without a good reason, Nick," he said, turning to face me.

I put my hand on his shoulder again and said, "Go to Staten Island, Vinnie. We'll talk tonight."

"Nick —"

"Go," I said, giving him a push. "Good luck."

As he started to walk to get into the car I called out, "Hey, where's Sister Olivia today?"

"She's not working in the Rectory today," he said. "Try the Convent."

I nodded, waited for him to pull out of the parking lot, then waved and started toward the Convent.

I rang the bell at the Convent, remembering the times as a boy in the mid-grades I'd been sent to the Convent to help Sister Michaela Tyson carry something to the school. The nuns I had in grammar school were stronger than most men I knew. Why is it that the things we remember most about the nuns we had in school are the right crosses and left hooks, the rulers across the knuckles, the time Sister Sugar Ray made one of the kids take off his pointed shoes — the ones with the illegal taps — and wear paper bags on his feet the rest of the day?

I couldn't imagine Sister Olivia striking a child, or even striking fear into a child's heart. That's what I remembered most about the nuns I had in school, being afraid of them.

Maybe the nuns didn't hit the parochial kids of today.

Lucky kids. I was still flinching years after I graduated from parochial school.

The door was opened by a nun in a habit. She was neither as pretty as Sister Olivia, nor as hard-looking as most of the nuns I remember. She had a remarkably smooth-skinned face, which made it very difficult to approximate her age.

"Yes?"

"Hi," I said, "I'd like to see Sister Olivia please?"

She regarded me benignly and asked, "Is there something I can help you with?"

"Uh, no, it's, uh, something, uh, personal." I was stammering. Were nuns allowed to have something personal?

"And your name?"

"Delvecchio, Nick Delvecchio."

Recognition lit up her eyes, and at that moment I'd have guessed her in her late twenties.

"Father Delvecchio's brother?" she said excitedly. "The private eye?"

"Uh, yep, that's me."

"Oh, come in, come in," she said, backing away from the door.

The farthest I had ever gotten into the Convent when I was a kid was a room just to the left of the front door. The Rectory and Convent were places of mystery when I was a kid.

"Wait here," she said, clasping her hands together in front of her. "I think Sister has just returned from her run."

She ran off into the dark recesses of the Rectory and I sat in a chair by the door and waited.

I could hear voices from inside the Convent, and three times different heads poked out and took a look at me.

My goodness, could it be I was the first private eye ever to enter this Convent?

"I'm sorry I kept you waiting," Sister Olivia said, entering the entry foyer. "I had to finish my cooling-down exercises."

I was staring, I knew I was staring, but I couldn't do anything about it. She was wearing light-blue running shorts and a dark-blue running top and — Jesus — she had a sports bra on underneath it. I remember as kids we used to wonder: *Do nuns wear bras? Do nuns have breasts? Do they have . . . nipples?* What was the one Jerry O'Brien had asked? Oh, yeah: *Do nuns shave their legs?*

Looking at Sister Olivia, I knew that the answer to all those things was *Yes.* The great mystery was solved. Jerry O'Brien had been my best friend in seventh and eighth grades. I wondered where he was now.

She had a towel around her neck, and

there were some sweat spots on the top, making it stick to her skin. The ends of her hair were wet, plastered to her forehead and neck. I could smell her sweat. There was a big sweat spot right between her breasts. *She smells just like a woman, Jerry,* I thought.

Okay, enough of that . . .

"Nick?"

"Hi," I said. "Remember what you said about wanting to help more if you could?"

"Yes, I remember."

"Do you still want to help?"

"Of course."

"Have lunch with me, Sister," I said. "I have to talk to you."

"Lunch?" She said it in a low voice, and then looked around as if to see if anyone had heard my invitation.

"This is on the up and up, Sister," I assured her. "I need your help in order to help Father Vinnie."

"Father Vinnie?" she said, and then giggled. "No one here calls him that. They call him Father Vincent, or Father Delvecchio. Father Vinnie . . . I like it."

"Sister? Lunch?"

She studied me for a moment — maybe she was trying to figure out if I was harmless or not — and then said, "Sure, I'll have lunch with you."

161

"Great!" I said, maybe with too much enthusiasm.

"I have to shower and change, and I have some errands to run."

"That's all right," I said. "We have time. I'll, uh, come back and get you at twelve o'clock."

"All right."

"I'll, uh, let myself out."

She smiled at me as I opened the door and stepped outside. It was quiet outside, but compared to the latent silence inside the Convent, it sounded positively loud. I could clearly hear the sound of children's voices coming from the school.

25

Once outside, I realized that I had three hours to kill. I found a pay phone across Rockaway Parkway and dialed the number for Long Island College Hospital. When the phone was answered, I asked for Linda Kellogg's room.

"Linda?" I said when she answered. "It's Nick Delvecchio."

"Oh . . . hi."

I don't have to be hit over the head with the obvious. The hesitation in her voice told me all I needed to know.

"Is he there?"

"Yes."

"When are you getting out?"

"Friday."

"That's good," I said. "I hope you're feeling better."

"Yes . . . much."

"All right," I said, "I won't keep you. I just want you to know that I'm still on the job."

"That's good."

"I'll talk to you soon."

"Fine. Good-bye."

Well, that killed all of five minutes. I was wondering if I should go and re-interview some of the PTA people when I realized that there was still one person I hadn't interviewed about Gloria Mancuso.

Monsignor Genovese.

I dialed the Rectory number. I knew the monsignor was in, but that didn't mean he'd have the time to see me or take the time.

When Mrs. Graf answered I asked for the monsignor.

"Who is calling?"

"Nick Delvecchio."

There was a long pause and then she said, "Weren't you just here?"

"Yes, I was."

There was another long pause and then she said, "Hold on."

"Mrs. Graf?"

"Y-yes?"

"Would you simply ask the monsignor if he could spare me some time this morning?"

"Of course," she said. "When may I tell him you would like to see him?"

"Oh . . . in about five minutes?"

Another puzzled pause and then: "I'll

164

check. Please hold."

I held for a couple of minutes and then Mrs. Graf came back on.

"You may come over anytime, Mr. Delvecchio. The monsignor can spare you some time."

"Thank you, Mrs. Graf."

I hung up and quickly crossed the street. As I walked toward the Rectory I saw that there was a florist's shop across the street. I hesitated a moment, then went across and bought a bunch of mixed flowers for Mrs. Graf. The poor woman probably thought Vinnie had been cursed with a deranged brother.

When she answered my knock I handed the flowers to her.

"For you."

"Oh . . . my," she said, accepting them. I could swear there were tears in her eyes. I guess Mr. Graf hadn't given her any flowers lately.

"Please come in," she said. "Monsignor is waiting for you."

She led me to the monsignor's office, the door of which was open.

"Monsignor? Mr. Delvecchio is here."

As I sidled on past her into the room I said, "You'd better get those into water."

"Yes . . . right away."

"Bribing my staff?" Monsignor asked.

"I confused the poor woman so much, I thought it was the least I could do."

"Frankly," he said, "I'm in somewhat the same state. What is it you want to say to me now that you could not have said earlier?"

"I had to make sure I spoke to my brother earlier, before he left. May I close the door?"

"Of course," he said, waving a hand negligently. "I don't have a lot of time, though. I have a meeting in . . . twenty minutes."

"I'll be brief, then," I promised, "and to the point. What can you tell me about Gloria Mancuso?"

His distaste showed on his face, but I didn't know if it was for the woman, or simply the subject.

"The woman is dead. What would you like me to tell you about her?"

I sat opposite him and said, "Anything you can tell me."

"I afraid I don't —"

"Let me ask you some questions, then. Were you aware of her flirtatious nature?"

"Mr. Delvecchio," he said, closing his eyes, "are you asking me if I knew Mrs. Mancuso was a tramp?"

"Monsignor!" I said, only half feigning shock. "That's a harsh word."

"People are what they are, Mr. Delvecchio," he said. "By not speaking of it, we don't change that. Yes, I knew what kind of woman Mrs. Mancuso was. Yes, I am aware that she has had affairs with some of the men whose children are in the school."

"Monsignor," I said, trying to hide my excitement, "could you give me any names?"

"No, I couldn't."

"Why not?" I asked. "This is to help my brother, Monsignor. If you could give me names —"

"I can't give you names because of where I got my information, Mr. Delvecchio."

"And where was that, Monsignor?"

"The confessional."

I stared at him for a moment, and then said, "Oh."

"Is there anything else I can do for you?"

I thought suddenly of the old talk-show host was it Mike Douglas? — who, when one of his guests started telling a story about someone he or she couldn't name, would ask, "Could you give us the initials?" I didn't think that would work with the monsignor.

"It was not my intention to strike you dumb, Mr. Delvecchio."

"Nevertheless, Monsignor . . ." I said.

There was a knock at a door, a different

door than the one through which I had entered, and it opened. A priest stepped into the room. He was tall and husky and looked to be about thirty-five or so, with curly dark hair.

"Oh, I'm sorry, Monsignor . . ."

"That's all right, Father," Monsignor said. "Father Kelleher? This is Nick Delvecchio."

"Ah, Father Delvecchio's brother," Father Kelleher said. He did not approach me, nor did he offer to shake hands. "A pleasure. Monsignor, you have a meeting in ten minutes."

"I know, Father, thank you."

Father Kelleher nodded, said, "Nice to have met you," to me, and left the same way he'd entered.

"Is there anything else, Mr. Delvecchio?"

"Yes, Monsignor," I said. "Do you think my brother was . . . indiscreet with Gloria Mancuso?"

"No, I do not," he said. "I have the highest respect for your brother, Mr. Delvecchio. I think that someday he will make a fine priest."

I couldn't help myself. I felt there was something unspoken in his reply.

"Just a fine priest?"

Monsignor stood up, preparing to leave.

He picked up what looked like a ledger book and tucked it beneath his arm.

"I don't know that he will ever progress further than that, Mr. Delvecchio. His handling of this . . . affair, for want of a better word, left much to be desired. Oh, I know how Mrs. Mancuso could bedevil men, and the Lord knows we're all just men, but I still feel he could have handled it . . . better. Now, if you will excuse me." He started for the side door Father Kelleher had used.

"One more thing, Monsignor."

"Mr. Delvecchio," he said in exasperation, "I've tried to be patient —"

"Has Mrs. Mancuso ever made sexual advances toward any other priest?"

"No!" he said, much too quickly and loudly. "If she had, I assure you I would know about it. None of my other priests has the same low regard for me that your brother obviously has. Now good day, sir!"

Without waiting for me to leave, he went out that side door.

Whoa, I thought. The monsignor was really prickly on the subject, and he was bitter as hell — pardon — at my brother for not having come to him. Maybe the monsignor felt that Vinnie had made him look bad to the Diocese by going over his head to them.

I had one brief moment where I was thinking about searching the monsignor's desk, then shook my head and got out of there.

26

"Mrs. Graf?" I said, poking my head into her office. The flowers were in a vase on her desk.

"Oh!" she said. "You startled me."

"I'm sorry. I wonder if you could help me."

She frowned, but said, "I'll try."

"How many priests are there here at the Church of the Holy Family?"

"Um, let me see . . . Father Kelleher . . . Father Macklin . . . um, Father Delvecchio, of course . . . Father Delbert —"

"Delbert?"

Mrs. Graf smiled for the first time since I'd met her, and shrugged.

". . . There's Father Sullivan and . . . Father Scanlon."

It struck me then that the Church and the Police Department had a lot in common. Many of their employees were Irish and Italian. Pop wasn't so right, after all.

"Are they all here now? I mean, for the past week, have they all been here?"

"Well, no," she said. "Father Scanlon is on retreat still, and Father Delbert had to go to Our Lady of Perpetual Faith — they are short-handed — um, I think that's it. The others have been here."

"Are either Father Macklin or Father Sullivan as young as Father Kelleher, or my brother?"

"Oh, no," she said, "Father Sullivan has been here for years, he's well into his seventies, and Father Macklin is about sixty, I believe."

"What about Father Delbert and Father Scanlon? How old are they?"

"Well, Father Delbert is in his forties, and Father Scanlon — that's hard to say. He's had a beard for so long, and there's some gray in it . . . and he is developing a bald spot . . . I suppose he's in his late forties."

"Thank you for your help, Mrs. Graf. I hope you have a very pleasant day."

"Why . . . thank you."

I went outside, juggling all of the priests' names and ages in my head. Certainly the monsignor, Father Macklin, and Father Sullivan were beyond Gloria Mancuso's range. That left Fathers Kelleher, Scanlon, and Delbert as . . . what? Say it, Nick. As suspects!

Just because my brother was true to his vows didn't mean all priests were.

A block away I found a McDonald's and

bought myself a cup of coffee. There was a pay phone right outside, and I used it to call Pop and Maria to arrange dinner at Pop's house.

"What'samatta?" Pop asked. "You invitin' yourself to dinner now?"

"I want to talk to you about something, Pop," I said. "Father Vinnie will be there, too."

"Fine," he said, "bring some Italian pastries . . ."

"Nick, you poop," my sister said. That's as close as she got to cursing these days. "You ran out the other night without telling me what's wrong with Father Vinnie."

I told her to be at Pop's tonight, and she'd hear it all. She wanted me to tell her on the phone, but I said no and hung up before she could think of something stronger to say to me.

I killed the rest of the time drinking coffee and juggling names . . .

I sat on the bottom two steps of the Rectory to wait the last ten minutes, watching kids play in the parking lot, which apparently also doubled as a playground. On the way there I had remembered that I was supposed to have lunch with Dominick

173

Barracondi. I also wanted to talk with Sister Olivia about who Gloria Mancuso's best friends were. So I decided to kill the proverbial two birds.

Wait until the Godfather found out whom I was bringing to lunch.

She took about twenty minutes, which was okay. I wasn't supposed to meet with Barracondi until 1 P.M. We could walk along Sheepshead Bay for a while and look at whatever fishing boats hadn't gone out yet.

When the door opened I stood up and turned around. I almost didn't recognize her because it was the first time I had seen her wearing her habit. It looked odd to me to see her in full dress uniform, with the headdress — or hood, or whatever they called it — the big white collar, the silver crucifix hanging around her neck, and the long string of brown rosary beads at her side.

She came down the steps and we stood staring at each other for a few moments. I thought she looked rather sad. I finally realized that she was trying to send me a message — and I got it. I wasn't to forget who she was.

"Okay," I said, finally finding my voice, "let's go."

"Where are we going to eat?"

"Sheepshead Bay."

"Sheepshead Bay?" she asked, surprised. "Why all the way over there?"

"Because," I said, "I'm going to introduce you to a real gangster."

"They don't really call them gangsters anymore, do they?"

Emmons Avenue is the real Sheepshead Bay. It's lined with restaurants and coffee shops, bait-and-tackle shops, fast-food restaurants, small grocery stores. When you reach the halfway point you see the docks, with all the fishing boats. It was afternoon now. The morning boats were returning, picking up the afternoon fishermen. Sometimes there were fishermen just fishing off the docks.

I had parked the car near Dominick Barracondi's restaurant, The Barge, and we were walking along the docks now. Right across the street were the seafood restaurants, pizza shops, sidewalk cafés, and ice-cream shops. When the weather was nice enough for walking, there were sidewalk flea markets set up. When the weather was really nice, in the spring and fall, there were people walking at all times of the day and night. In the summer, people walked at night.

Behind all the stores and shops were the bungalows. Once, this had been a beautiful place to live, right near the beach. Now families were living in tiny bungalows because they couldn't sell them. There were rows of them behind the stores and the main streets, some of them separated only by small walkways with grandiose names.

But to the question of gangsters.

"There are so many different names, and they change all the time," I said. "Now they call them wise guys."

"Wise guys? Why?"

"Because somebody decided it was a likely name."

"Isn't that a TV show?"

"You have TV in the Convent?"

"Of course," she said. "What do you think, we're in the Middle Ages?"

A nun walking along Emmons Avenue was not an everyday occurrence. We were drawing looks. I checked my watch.

"Let's start back," I said. "By the time we reach the restaurant, it'll be time to go in."

"This man, Dominick . . ."

"Barracondi," I said. "When he was younger, they called him Nicky Barracuda."

"He's actually your godfather?"

"Yes."

"Were you named after him?"

"No," I said, "he's Dominick, and I'm Nicholas. He and my father were friends, but my mother didn't like him, so they compromised. They named him my godfather, but didn't name me after him."

"But you're both called Nick, or Nicky?"

"Nobody calls him Nicky Barracuda anymore," I said. "Remember that."

"And you?" she asked playfully. "Who calls you Nicky?"

"Only my family," I said. "My father and my sister."

"Not Father?"

"No."

"Can I call you Nicky?"

I hesitated, then said, "No."

We were a few blocks from the restaurant when I said, "Sister, I've got to ask you some questions you might not want to answer."

"Shoot."

I gave her a look and she smiled.

"First, I need to know who Gloria Mancuso's best friends were."

"Friends?" she said. "Gloria didn't have friends. She had admirers. Men admired her because she was beautiful, and women admired her because she . . . well, because they wished they could be like her. Of course, at the same time they hated her for what she was."

"A tramp."

She looked at me and said, "Who told you that?"

"Monsignor."

"Really?" She was shocked. I decided not to tell her what he'd said about the confessional. Somehow, I didn't think his mentioning it to me was . . . kosher.

"Sister, what about the other priests?"

"What about them?"

"Do you think Gloria ever made . . . sexual advances to them?"

She smiled and for a moment I thought she might laugh out loud.

"What?"

"I was just thinking of Gloria Mancuso chasing Father Sullivan or Father Macklin."

"What about the others? Father Delbert?"

"No," she said with assurance.

"Why not?"

"He's a dear man, but he's also the homeliest man I've ever met. No, I think Gloria, if she had approached a priest, would have chosen your brother, or Father Kelleher. The Sisters generally consider your brother the best-looking priest in the Diocese."

It was my turn to be surprised.

"You . . . Sisters talk about things like that?"

Sheepishly, she said, "Some of us do." After a moment she put her hand on my arm, looked at me and said, "Nick, did she . . ."

"Did she what?"

"Make advances toward Father Vincent?"

"She did," I said. "The police are suspicious of him."

"Can they really suspect him of . . . of killing her?" she asked, in shock.

"They can," I said, "and they do."

"Would they really . . . arrest him?"

"They might."

"Oh, my . . . I knew there was something wrong, but I didn't know it was this bad. Nick, what can I do to help Father Vincent?"

"You're doing it, Sister," I said, "you're doing it."

27

I spotted Benny the Card as soon as we entered the restaurant. He wasn't hard to spot. He was about eight feet across at the shoulders, dressed in a tux and flashing a pinky ring on each hand. Since he had gone from button man to maître d', he'd put on about fifty pounds, most of it in the gut. His real name was Benvenuto Cardone, and we had gone to high school together.

"Aye, Nicky D," he said, coming over.

He came over and shook my hand, then nodded to Sister Olivia and said, "Good afternoon, Sister."

"Sister Olivia, this is Benny Cardone. Benny, would you tell the Don we're here?"

"Nick, I know the Don's expectin' you, but . . ."

"Just set another place at the table, Benny. Okay?"

"Sure, Nick," he said, looking confused. "Just let me tell the boss you're here."

While Benny went and told Nicky Barracuda about the extra guest, Sister Olivia looked the place over.

"What do you think?" I asked.

"It looks very nice," she said, "and the smells are heavenly — no pun intended."

"That's the Don's sauce you smell," I said. "It's his own recipe."

"Nick . . . is this place . . ."

"Legit? Sure, it's legit. This is Dominick's baby."

"What about Benny?"

"Benny the Card," I said. "Since he's gone legit, he's put on a ton."

"What did he do before he went legit?"

"Sister," I said, "you don't want to know."

Benny came back and said, "All set, paesan. Follow me."

"Sister," I said. She followed Benny, and I followed her.

Dominick Barracondi had a table set up in his office, and there were three chairs.

"Nicholas," he said, spreading his arms. "Welcome. I'm glad you came."

There was no denying that Dominick Barracondi was an elegant man. His hair was snow-white, as was his carefully trimmed mustache. He looked like an Italian Cesar Romero.

"Hello, Godfather."

He looked pleased when I called him that, but I did it for Sister Olivia's benefit. I wanted her to remember this afternoon.

"I didn't expect you to bring a friend, though." He must have been going crazy wondering what I was up to, but I had to hand it to him, he didn't miss a beat.

"I want you to meet my friend, Sister Olivia."

"Sister," Barracondi said, "it's an honor to have you in my restaurant."

"Thank you, Mr. Barracondi."

"Please, sit here," he said, holding a chair out for her.

"Nicholas?"

I sat across from Sister Olivia, and he sat between us.

"Benny," he said then, "tell Carlo to serve lunch."

Lunch consisted of linguine with white clam sauce, followed by eggplant parmigiana, fried zucchini, and garlic bread. I had to give Dominick Barracondi credit, he had one of the best Italian kitchens in New York City.

"This is wonderful, Mr. Barracondi," Sister Olivia said to him. "This must be the best Italian restaurant in Brooklyn."

"Well, unfortunately, we are not yet considered the best. There is a restaurant just a few blocks from here which has a long history here in Sheepshead Bay, and that one is generally considered the best

182

Italian restaurant in Brooklyn."

"What restaurant is that?"

"It is called Maria's. I have eaten there myself, and the food is excellent. Still, I hope that someday my own humble establishment will be able to match their fine reputation."

We had dessert — fresh peaches soaked in vermouth, something he admitted he had "borrowed" from Maria's — and coffee, and then he said to Sister Olivia, "Sister, if you do not mind, I would like a few moments alone with my godson?"

"Oh, of course," she said, standing up. "I'll wait outside."

"Benny will see to your comfort," Barracondi said, and Benny nodded. He had been standing faithfully by the door throughout lunch, hands clasped in front of him.

"This way, Sister," he said, allowing her to precede him. I had never seen Benny act like such a gentleman before.

My godfather refilled our coffee cups and then sat back in his chair, regarding me with a somewhat critical expression on his face.

"So, Nick?"

"So . . . what?"

"Why have you and your brother not asked for my help?"

"I beg your pardon?"

"Do not play games with me," he said. "I know that Father Vincent is that much removed from being arrested." He was holding his thumb and forefinger about an inch apart.

"How do you know about it?"

He shrugged.

"How do I know about anything? I hear things."

"*What* do you know about it?"

"Only what I have heard," he said, "that Father Vincent is suspected of killing a woman he may have had an affair with. Both are inconceivable."

"I know that," I said. "What have you done?"

"I? I have done nothing. I have not been asked to intervene. Does your father know?"

"No."

"Ah," he said, as if he understood, "your father would have asked for my help."

"He'll be told tonight."

"And your sister?"

"She, too, but they won't be asking for your help. Neither will I."

"And why not?"

"That will be up to Father Vinnie, and you know how he feels about taking help from you."

Vinnie has been adamant his entire adult life about not taking help from Dominick Barracondi. I've never approved of my god-father, but I have been known to bend the rules from time to time. Not Vinnie, though.

"Your brother is a stubborn man."

"Tell me about it."

"And a proud one."

I knew that, too. That was why I hated seeing what this was doing to him.

"You must tell him, Nicholas, to come to me for help. I cannot help unless he asks."

I'll give the old man credit for that. Even last year, when Maria was on a hijacked plane, as badly as he wanted to help, he did nothing, because we didn't ask him to. He stuck to his guns, or his code, of not inter-fering unless specifically asked to.

"I don't think we'll be needing your help," I said, "but we appreciate the offer."

"I know an excellent attorney."

"We have an excellent attorney."

"A *Spanish* attorney."

"Heck Delgado is Mexican."

He flinched, as if I'd struck him.

"You must talk to your brother —"

"My brother is his own man. I can't make him do anything he doesn't want to do."

"You underestimate your influence with

Father Vincent," he said. "After all, he did come to you, and he has done as you say up to now, hasn't he?"

Damn him. Where was his contact, in the police or in the Church?

"Thank you for lunch, Don Dominick."

"Ah!" he exploded, rising and throwing his napkin down onto the table. Benny must have been right by the door because he was inside in a flash, his hand dipping into his jacket. He still moved well for a big man.

He stared at Barracondi for a sign, and the older man simply waved him away irritably, then turned his attention back to me. Benny backed out of the room.

"I love your family as if it were my own, Nicholas, and yet you spurn me at every turn. Last year I could have helped your sister."

"You would have gotten her killed."

"Do you know what I could have done for your career in the Police Department? You could be a lieutenant by now; all you had to do was ask."

I didn't reply. I had always wondered if he had done something five years ago to keep me out of jail. It would have been against his code, but . . .

"Do you know what I could have done for your brother over the years?" he went on.

"He could be pastor of his own parish right now. A monsignor! In time, I could make him the youngest bishop in the history of the Church, and after that, a cardinal."

"Could you make him Pope?"

He stared at me and then said, "There are limits even to what I can do, Nicholas."

I was a little surprised to hear him admit that.

"Then you've got nothing to offer him," I said. "Thank you for lunch. The Sister and I appreciated it. It was excellent, as usual."

"Nick!"

"Yes?"

I don't know what he was going to say, but instead he said, "Tell your friend, Sister Olivia, that it was a pleasure to meet her."

"I'll tell her."

I left his office and found Sister Olivia sitting at a table nearby. Benny was standing right outside the door, and obviously had been throughout our conversation.

"Hey, Nicky," he said, putting his hand on my arm, "what's with you and the Don?"

"Don't worry about it, Benny."

"He just wants to help."

"I know," I said. "I know he does. Just don't worry about it, all right? It's not your concern."

I started for Sister Olivia and Benny

moved his hand from my hand to my chest.

"Nicky," he said slowly, "you hurt the Don and you and me, we're gonna go round and round." He used a sausage-like forefinger on his other hand to make little circles in the air.

I put my hand against his chest, meaning to say something, but then just patted him there and walked to Sister Olivia. She had been watching Benny and me with eyes as big as saucers.

"Come on, Sister," I said, putting my hand out to her. "I'll get you back to the Convent."

28

Sister Olivia was quiet for most of the ride back to the Convent. In fact, she didn't speak again until I had pulled into the parking lot.

"Benny," she said, "he wouldn't actually . . . hurt you, would he?"

"Benny?" I said, with disdain for the idea. "Benny's a pussycat."

"When you and he were . . . standing there . . . looking at each other, I thought . . ."

"Benny and I went to school together, Sister," I said, cutting her off. "I've been dealing with him for years, and he hasn't broken me in half yet." I put my hand on hers on the seat and said, "Don't worry."

I didn't bother telling her about the time, in my junior year, Benny broke my arm to teach me a lesson. I had been looking at his girl. Back then Benny had been a football player and a bodybuilder. Over the years, his body lost the definition it once had, but he never lost his great strength. Even that afternoon, when he put his hand on my chest, I could feel his strength.

"When the two of you were staring at each other, I thought you were going to say something."

"I was," I said, "but Benny was only displaying his loyalty to the Don." I looked up and saw three children at a window watching us. Two girls and a boy. I waved and they giggled. Sister Olivia looked up, craning her neck to see through the windshield, waved, and they giggled some more and waved back.

I think we both realized at the same time that my hand was still on hers. She slowly removed it and said, "Well, thanks for lunch. It was . . . interesting."

"I hope it was," I said. "I hope you enjoyed it, Sister."

"Well," she said, "it wasn't like anything I've read or seen in the movies. Consequently, yes, I did enjoy it quite a bit."

She opened her door and stepped out, and I opened mine, got out and looked over the roof at her.

"If you think of anything else you might tell me about Gloria Mancuso, please let me know."

"Are you going to talk to her husband?"

"I'd like to," I said. "I've just got to come up with a good enough excuse."

We stared at each other over the roof for a

few moments, and I noticed what pretty brown eyes she had. Eyes that were very pretty, even without makeup.

"Well," she said, "I've got to get back."

"I'll see ya."

"Yes," she said. She started to turn, then said, "Oh, wait, wait . . ."

"What?"

"I just thought of something. Gloria bowled."

"What?"

"She was in a bowling league, at that bowling alley named after the baseball player."

I knew the one she meant, in Mill Basin, on Stillwell Avenue.

"You might be able to find a best friend there."

"Yeah," I said, "I might. Thanks, Sister."

"You're welcome."

"You're a great assistant detective."

"Thanks. Bye."

"Good-bye."

She started to walk away, then stopped and turned back to face me.

"There's something I have to ask you," she said.

"Go ahead." I thought I knew what it was going to be, and I was right.

"Why did you take me with you today, to

see Mr. Barracondi?"

I'd been asking myself the same question.

"Would you believe I was just killing two birds with one stone, seeing him and taking you to lunch?"

"I'm afraid I wouldn't."

"I didn't think so."

"Perhaps I can make it easy on you," she said. "It was rather obvious to me that you don't have the feelings for your godfather that he has for you."

"My problem starts right there," I said honestly. "How can he have led the life he did and have feelings for anyone?"

"He obviously thinks highly of you, and is hurt by the fact that you don't return his feelings."

I frowned.

"I think you took me as an act of defiance against him. I mean, it does seem rather odd to take a nun to lunch with a Mafia Don, doesn't it?"

"I suppose you're right," I said. "It is odd, and I do and say a lot of stupid things when it comes to dealing with . . . him. I'm sorry, Sister."

"Don't apologize," she said. "I'm rather pleased with myself that I figured it out."

"You really are a great assistant detective."

She smiled and turned to walk away.

I watched her walk across the parking lot, and as I watched I saw something beyond her. It was a car . . . a shiny blue car.

"Sister!"

She stopped and turned, frowning. I trotted after her.

"Do you know whose car that is?" I asked when I reached her.

She turned to look where I was pointing and said, "It belongs to the Church."

"What does that mean?" I asked. "Anybody can drive it?"

"No, not anybody," she said, "There are cars for the use of the Sisters, like that station wagon . . . and then cars for the use of the priests, and then a car for the monsignor."

"Well, who uses that one?"

"I believe I've seen the priests driving that one."

"What priests?"

"Um, I've seen Father Sullivan drive it, and Father Kelleher, and . . . Father Delvecchio."

"Vinnie?"

"Nick, I'm sure they've all driven it at one time or another. Is it important?"

"Maybe," I said, "and maybe there are just a lot of shiny blue cars in the city."

She didn't know what I was talking about, and I didn't take the time to fill her in. We said good-bye again and I walked back to my car. When I got in I looked up at the school and those same kids were watching me from the window. I was wondering why they were there and not at their desks when a nun came up behind them and obviously shooed them away, back to their seats. She looked down at me and frowned, and I saw that she was the spitting image of the kind of nun I had when I was in parochial school.

I drove away, feeling that maybe things weren't so different these days, after all.

29

After leaving Sister Olivia I decided to drive right to the bowling alley to check on that lead. I didn't know when Gloria Mancuso's league bowled, during the day or the evening, but it was still early enough for a day league to be in progress. Maybe I could find something out.

The noise in the bowling alley was almost deafening. It seemed that every alley in the place was taken, and my ears were assailed with the sound of rolling balls and falling pins.

I walked up to the desk and the man behind it told me, "No open lanes, Mac."

"I'm not interested in bowling."

"No? Well, you can't be here for the food."

"I'd like to talk to someone about a league."

"Men's league bowls at night."

"I'm interested in the women's leagues."

"Sure you are. You seen some of these women bowlers?"

"Have you?"

"You bet I have. Ain't but one or two of

them worth standing behind while they're bowling. I mean, they're nice ladies, but . . ."

"Maybe you can help me," I said. "You seem to be a man who notices things."

He puffed his chest up and said, "Well, yeah, I keep my eyes open."

"There's a woman who bowls in a league here, but I don't know which one it is."

"What's her name?"

"Mancuso," I said, "Gloria Mancuso. She's a blonde, very attractive —"

He held up his hand to stop me.

"Save it, Mac. Everybody here knows Gloria. She's that exception I was talkin' about. Whoa, is that gal a looker, or what?"

"She's dead."

His jaw dropped and he said, "What?"

"Somebody killed her."

"Aw, no," he said, as if he had been related to her.

"Did you know her well?"

"Naw," he said, "not that I didn't try, but I wasn't her type, you know?"

"You seem pretty upset —"

"Hey, man," he said, "just seeing her walk in here on Thursday night was worth all the shit I got to go through all the other nights and days."

"That's when she bowled? Thursday night?"

"Yeah. Last year she bowled two nights, but this year she cut back to one. Something about the PTA, I think."

"She have many friends?"

"Who knows, man. I watch these women here, and I don't know if they're friends or not. One day they're talkin', another day they ain't. It's easier with the guys, you know? You can tell who hates whose guts, but the women are different. You know what I mean?"

"Yeah, I think I do."

"You a cop?"

"Why didn't you ask me that before?"

" 'Cause you didn't look like a cop, then."

"And I do now?"

He grinned and said, "There's somethin' about a man who's askin' questions that changes the way he looks."

"I used to be a cop," I said, "I'm private now."

"That explains it."

"Well, thanks for the information."

"It's a shame about that blonde," he said, shaking his head. "I got to find me a new fantasy now."

"Life is hard . . ."

I borrowed Hacker's car that night to drive to my father's house. I hadn't heard from Heck or from Vinnie, so I guessed we'd all find out at the same time what had happened at the police station in Staten Island.

I did manage to talk to Sam before leaving.

"How do you look in bowling shoes?"

"What?"

I told her about Gloria Mancuso's Thursday-night bowling league, and explained how I had to go to my father's house with Vinnie to break the news to him and Maria.

"What would I have to do?"

"Ask questions," I said. "Make like you're there looking for her. Get some of the women to talk about her."

"Will they know she's dead?"

"I don't know, but it doesn't matter. Either way, she's the kind of woman who inspires gossip."

"All right," she said, then frowned and asked, "I won't have to bowl, will I?"

"Why?"

"I've never bowled."

"Don't worry about it," I said. "Just wear a short skirt and look athletic. They won't have any open lanes, anyway."

"This is great, Nick. Thanks for giving me another chance to help you. Uh, what about Linda Kellogg?"

"She's being released tomorrow afternoon. I'll try to get in touch with her in the afternoon."

"And how are things going with your brother?"

"I don't know," I said. "I'll find out tonight when I see him."

"Knock on my door when you come home, all right?"

"You might be asleep."

"No, I won't," she said. "Besides, I have the feeling you'll need to talk."

"You might be right," I said. "Okay, I'll knock."

She touched my arm and said, "Good luck . . ."

On the way to the house I thought about what Barracondi had said to me that afternoon. Maybe I was being too stubborn; after all, it wasn't my neck that hung in the balance, but Vinnie's. If Dominick Barracondi could bail him out of this jam, then why not let him? I decided to talk to Vinnie seriously about asking for help.

When I reached the house I couldn't park right in front because there was already a car there — a shiny blue car. I frowned, drove on ahead about two or three houses and found a spot. When I walked back I examined the car more closely and discovered that it was the same one I had seen earlier in the school parking lot. Vinnie must have driven it here. I didn't know what car Vinnie had driven to Pop's earlier that week, and I didn't know which car he'd driven to my apartment the night we met Heck.

I went up the walk to the front door, found that it was unlocked, and went inside.

"Anybody home?" I called out.

Maria and Vinnie came out of the kitchen.

"It's about time," Maria said, putting her hands on her trim hips. "Maybe now we can find out what's going on."

"Hello, Nick."

"Vinnie," I said. "How're you doing?"

"Okay."

"And why shouldn't he be doing okay?" Maria demanded.

"Is that your sauce I smell?" I asked her.

"It certainly is, and it's left over from the other night."

"That doesn't mean it can't burn."

She turned on her heel and stalked into the kitchen, leaving me and Vinnie alone.

"Where's Pop?" I asked.

"In his room."

"Did you tell him?"

"I was waiting for you."

"What happened in Staten Island?"

"Well," he said, "I'm not under arrest."

"Dinner's ready," Maria said, sticking her head out of the kitchen.

"When should I tell them?" Vinnie asked me.

"After dinner, Vinnie," I said, putting my hand on his arm, "after dinner."

We went in to have dinner, and I didn't envy my brother the task ahead of him.

"That's-a crazy!"

That was my father's reaction to the news. Sometimes when he gets upset, his English acquires just a slight Italian accent. Maria, on the other hand, just sort of sat stunned.

"How could they think that a priest — my son! — could even-a think such a thing?"

"Pop," Vinnie said, "they only see me as a man, not as a priest."

"Well, you didn't know this woman, did you, Father?"

It always struck me odd to hear my father call my brother "Father."

"Yes, Pop, I did know her. She was a parent, and a parishioner. She was president of the PTA."

"Yeah, but you know a lot of parents. They gonna arrest you every time one of them gets killed?"

"Pop," Vinnie said, "she was an attractive woman — she was a *beautiful* woman —"

"You ain't supposed to notice things like that!" Pop snapped.

"Pop, I'm a priest, but I'm not dead."

"Don't talk-a like that!"

"Pop," Maria said, "stop it."

My father looked at her in surprise.

"Vinnie, do you have a lawyer?"

"Yes."

"Who?"

"His name is Hector Delgado."

"A Puerto Rican?" my father said. "An Italian lawyer is-a no good enough-a for you?"

"He's not Puerto Rican, Pop," Vinnie said, "he's Mexican."

"That's-a worse."

"Pop —" Vinnie said.

"Pop —" Maria said.

"Stop!" I said, louder than everyone else. "Just stop it!"

They all looked at me.

"Vinnie might be in a lot of trouble," I said, "and he needs some understanding and support from his family."

"But the cops can't be serious about this," Pop said. "He's a priest, for Chrissake, they can't think he killed somebody."

"They do, Pop," I said, "that's why he and the lawyer went to see the detectives today."

"And what happened?" Maria asked.

"Let's give him a chance to tell us."

So we all kept quiet and he told us about it . . .

30

When Heck and Vinnie reached the one-two-two they announced themselves at the desk. Rather than being sent up on their own, as I was, the desk officer called ahead and Detective Giambone came down to get them. Vinnie described Giambone as medium height but well-built, with his hair perfectly in place and his suit, shirt, and tie perfectly matched. He sounded like a perfect match for his partner.

Upstairs, they spoke to both Detective Lacy and Detective Giambone.

Basically, the detectives wanted to know about Vinnie's relationship with Gloria Mancuso. Heck, who knew the whole story, had instructed Vinnie to tell them everything. Vinnie did, right up to the point where he left the Holiday Inn by the side door and drove back to the Rectory.

"Now let's get this straight," Lacy said when he was done. "You're saying that this woman undressed completely, and you just left the room?"

"That's right."

Lacy looked at his partner, who formed a soundless whistle with his lips.

"I understand Mrs. Mancuso was an extremely beautiful woman," Lacy said. "Of course, I've only seen her corpse, but . . ."

"Yes," Vinnie said, "she was extremely beautiful."

"And there she was, butt-naked," Giambone said, "and you just walked out?"

"I said that," Vinnie replied. "After all, I am a priest."

"Yes, you did say that," Lacy said. "My partner is just such a pussyhound that he finds it hard to believe even of a priest, Mr. Delvecchio."

"Father," Heck said at that point.

"I beg your pardon?" Lacy said.

"My client is cooperating fully," Heck said. "I would like him afforded the respect he deserves. His name is *Father* Delvecchio."

"Excuse me . . . Father," Lacy said, "but by cooperating fully that would mean that you were telling us the whole truth, and frankly, we're not all that sure you are."

"What is it you think my client is lying about?" Heck asked.

Lacy and Giambone exchanged a glance and Giambone nodded.

"We think he had sex with Mrs. Mancuso."

"When?" Heck asked.

"Well," Lacy said, "we believe that he had an affair with her, but we also believe that he had sex with her the night she was killed, in the Holiday Inn."

"I didn't," Vinnie said, his heart pounding, "I never did! That would have meant breaking my vows."

"You mean no priest has ever broken his vows?" Giambone asked.

"There have been cases, yes," Vinnie said, "but I have never broken mine."

"Counselor," Lacy said, "we can solve this question easily — at least, the question of whether or not he had sex with her that night."

"What do you suggest?"

"We'd like Father Delvecchio to submit to a blood test, so we can type it to the semen we found in Gloria Mancuso's vagina."

"She had a pussyful," Giambone said, grinning. Vinnie thought that Giambone was trying to work on his head from the moment he arrived there.

Heck and Vinnie were allowed a few moments to talk over the proposal. Heck took Vinnie out into the hall rather than talk alone in the room. They decided that Vinnie would take the test, because he had nothing to hide. A semen test couldn't prove that he *did* do it, only that he *couldn't* have done it. If the semen didn't type as his, that worked for them, and if it *was* his type, it was still inconclusive. The detectives gave them the name and address of a lab there in Staten Island, where they could stop and have it done before they returned to Brooklyn . . .

"On the way out," Vinnie said, "we saw Mr. Mancuso and his lawyer."

"Did he say anything to you?" I asked.

"Yes," Vinnie said, "he said he hoped I burned in hell for killing his wife."

"That's-a crazy," my father said, throwing his hands up in the air.

"His being there," I said, "means that he's still a suspect, too."

"There," Pop said, "her husband killed her. It happens all-a the time."

"Nick," Maria said, "what happens if Vinnie's blood type matches the, uh . . . what happens if it matches?"

"It still won't be conclusive," I said. "There are a lot of people who would match — I would, for instance."

"Yes," Vinnie said, "but you didn't know her. I did."

"Would that be enough to arrest him?" Maria asked.

I hesitated a moment, then looked at Vinnie and asked, "What did Heck say?"

"He said that if there was a match he thought they would talk to the DA about arresting me, but it was still inconclusive."

"Then they wouldn't arrest him? They couldn't." Maria argued.

"Not just on that, Maria," Nick said, "but they have a lot more. First, Vinnie knew the victim; second, a lot of people know what kind of woman Gloria was. It's no secret that she flirted with Vinnie, among others; third, her husband probably told the police something about Vinnie, but most damaging is that Vinnie admitted he was at the hotel that night, and in her room."

"That's-a the lawyer's fault," Pop said. "You should-a got an Italian lawyer. Don Dominick could have helped us with that."

"No, Pop," Vinnie said. "We are not going to Dominick Barracondi. That's final."

"Let's not argue about that now," I said, cutting off any reply from my father. "Maria, why don't you clear off the table for coffee."

"Where are you going?" she asked.

"I have to make a call," I said, getting up. "Pop, I'm going to use the phone in your room."

I went into Pop's room to use the phone

208

there, and dialed Heck Delgado's home number.

"I'm glad you called," Heck said when he answered. "I want you to talk to Gloria Mancuso's husband."

"That's what I was calling you about," I said. "Normally I wouldn't do that in an open homicide investigation."

"Your license will be safe, as you are representing me. Technically, we're not investigating the murder, we're simply preparing a defense for our client, in the event he's arrested."

"Fine," I said, "I'll go and see Mancuso tomorrow."

"Keep in touch."

"Nick, what happened to that information from the desk clerk on the key?"

"I don't know," I said, "but I intend to find out. He might have found himself a better place for the information."

"Let me know what happens."

"You got it."

I hung up and heard the raised voices in the kitchen. I shook my head and walked toward them.

". . . have you be so damned stubborn," my father was saying.

"And where do you think I got that from, Pop?"

"Please," Maria said, "don't fight . . ." I could tell from her voice that she was close to tears.

They all fell silent as I entered the room.

"Vinnie, can we talk?"

"You can't talk in front of us?" Pop demanded.

"I want to talk, Pop, not argue."

Vinnie came with me into the living room.

"What is it, Nick?"

"The car you drove here."

"The Chevy?"

"The shiny blue one out front. How often do you drive it?"

"I don't know," he said. "Whenever it's available, I guess. If no one else is using it."

"What about that night? Did you use it that night?"

"No," he said, "I used the Ford. Why?"

"I told you that the desk clerk said she was dropped off? Well, she got out of a shiny blue car."

"Oh . . ." he said, realizing what that meant. "All the detectives have to do is check and see what cars we use at the church, and they'll have another nail for my coffin."

"I want you to do something for me," I said. "Find out where that car was that night. If it was being used, find out who was using it."

"I can do that."

"Okay," I said. "Listen, I'm gonna leave now. Why don't you do the same?"

He smiled and said, "I can't do that."

"Pop's gonna stay on you, Vinnie."

"He's worried, Nick, and so is Maria. I'll stay for a while."

"Suit yourself."

"What are you going to do tomorrow?"

"I've got a couple of things to do. I've got to go and see Gloria's husband, and then I've got to find that hotel clerk."

"Stay in touch, okay? If they arrest me, I — I want to be able to find you."

I touched his arm and said, "I'll keep checking in, Vinnie."

31

As promised, I knocked on Sam's door when I returned, even before going to my own apartment. When she opened the door I smelled coffee. She was wearing a T-shirt that said BROOKLYN, WHERE THE WEAK ARE KILLED AND EATEN.

"Is that for me?" I asked.

"The coffee is."

"That's what I meant."

"Come on in."

I stepped inside. Sam's apartment is set up exactly the same way mine is, but hers always looks and feels better. The room I use as an office is her bedroom. I use it as an office because mine has a door to the hall. Hers does not. The room that is my bedroom is her office.

"Sit down and tell me how it went at your father's," she said, pouring two cups of coffee.

"Oh, it didn't go well," I said. "Pop *did* react pretty well, but he was pissed."

"What about your sister?"

"She was real quiet."

She put the coffee in front of me and sat

across from me. Neither one of us used milk or sugar.

"You know what amazes me?"

"What?" I asked.

"That something like this, and what happened to your sister last year, could happen to the same family."

"Yeah," I said, "well, I guess we haven't had a lot of luck of late."

"That's putting it mildly."

"Never mind that," I said. "Did you go bowling?"

"You shit!" she said, reaching over and punching me in the arm.

"What's that for?"

"You didn't warn me about the lech."

"You must mean my friend behind the desk."

"Greasy-looking guy with dark hair?"

"That's him," I said. "He was real disappointed about Gloria being killed. He said he was gonna have to find a new fantasy."

"Well, I didn't apply for the job."

"Did you talk to the women?"

"I sure did," she said, grinning. "Boy, they had a lot to say about Gloria. Half of them liked her, and the other half hated her but envied her."

"That's the reaction I got from the PTA, too."

In general, the women in the bowling league told Sam just what the women in the PTA had told me.

"You didn't find a best friend?"

"No," she said, "there didn't seem to be any such animal. One woman went so far as to say that Gloria was her own best friend."

"And worst enemy."

"Not much help, huh?"

"You did fine, Sam," I said, touching her knee. "Thanks for going."

"What else did you do today?"

"I had lunch with a nun."

"What?"

I told her about lunch with Sister Olivia and Dominick Barracondi.

"What's with the nun, Nick?"

"She's helping me."

"Is she pretty?"

"Well, yeah, she's pretty."

"Uh-huh."

"Well, the first time I met her she wasn't wearing her habit. How was I supposed to know she was a nun?"

"Uh-huh," she said again.

"Besides, she's given me some information on Gloria Mancuso."

"Like what?"

"Well, she gave me the bowling-alley

lead. It's not her fault it didn't pan out."

"Of course not."

I stood up and said, "Cut it out, Sam. She's a nun."

"I didn't say anything," she said, all wide-eyed innocence.

"It's what you were thinking," I said.

"How do you know what I'm thinking?"

"It shows in your eyes," I said. "I'm going home before your dirty mind contaminates me."

"Ha!" she snapped as I made for the door. "Me contaminate *you?*"

I crossed the hall and entered my apartment through my office. My one-eyed friend wasn't blinking any messages at me, so I sat down and dialed the Holiday Inn in Staten Island. I was going to try to bluster my way to the information I wanted.

"I'd like to speak to Riley, please," I said when the phone was answered by a woman.

"Riley's not on tonight."

"Is this the operator?"

"Yes."

"This is Detective Giambone from the one-two-two. I'm investigating the murder that happened there Saturday night."

"Oh yes, that was terrible," she said.

"Yes, it was," I said. "Listen, you could

help me out of a jam."

"If I can, I'd like to," she said. She sounded very young, and I was already changing my tactics in mid-stream.

"Riley gave me his home address, and I lost it. I really have to talk to him tomorrow morning. Could you help me?"

"Gee, I don't know," she said. "I don't think I'm allowed to do that."

"Aw, come on," I said. "If you do it for me, I'll send you some flowers."

"Really?"

"When's the last time a man sent you flowers?"

"Oh, a boy has never sent me flowers." Now I knew she was young, because she said "boy" rather than "man."

"What's your name?"

"Tina."

"Tina, nobody's ever sent you flowers?"

"No."

"I can't believe that," I said. "You have such a sexy voice."

"Really? Well, I'm afraid I'm a little overweight."

"Ooh, I like women with meat on their bones," I said. "Listen, Tina, I'll send you a whole bunch of flowers if you help me out just this once."

"Well . . . I could give you his phone

number. Would that be enough?"

"Honey, listen," I said. "I'm a policeman. If you give me his phone number, I can find out his address, but why make me go through all that?"

"Well," she said, coming around, "when you put it that way, it does sort of make sense."

"And nobody'll ever know," I said. "Imagine what your co-workers are gonna think when you get dozens of roses in the mail."

"Dozens?"

"Dozens."

"All right . . . Detective Giambone, is it?"

"That's right."

"Hold on . . ."

I held on for a few minutes, and then she came back on.

"He lives in Brooklyn," she said, sounding surprised.

"Really? I would have thought he'd live in Staten Island since he works there."

"I know, I live in Staten Island."

"Is that so?"

"Yes."

There was a pause, and I knew she was waiting for "Detective Giambone" to ask for her phone number or address. I wondered just how overweight poor Tina was.

"Where in Brooklyn does he lives, Tina?"

"Bay Ridge," she said, "just across the bridge." She gave me his address on Third Avenue, in the Eighties. I knew that area was mostly shops, restaurants and the like, with apartments in the back and over the stores. I was pleased that I wouldn't have to drive out to Staten Island to see him.

"Since you have it there, Tina, how about giving me his phone number, too?"

"Sure," she said, reeling it off.

"Tina, can you tell me one more thing?"

"Sure."

"When was he at work last?"

"I saw him here last night."

"Was he there today?"

"He was off tonight."

"What about tomorrow?"

"He should be off tomorrow, too. I guess he'll be back Saturday night."

"Okay, thanks, honey. You watch for those flowers, okay?"

"I work nights. I start at eleven."

"I'll get them there early, so you can enjoy them all night."

"Thanks," she said. "Oh, if you work nights, maybe we could, you know, have coffee?"

I felt like a heel when I said, "I'll call you, Tina. Okay?"

"Okay," she said happily.

I hung up, making a mental note to remember to send her those flowers, anyway, even if I wasn't Detective Giambone.

32

I still had the list of PTA officers that Sister Olivia had given me, and right at the top was Gloria Mancuso's address. I didn't know what Anthony Mancuso did for a living, so I didn't know when he'd be home. I decided to try and catch him at the school.

At eight-fifteen I was parked in the school parking lot. On other days I had noticed that a good portion of the students entered from the Flatlands Avenue side of the school, and they looked like the older kids. Since Mancuso's daughter was in her last year, I assumed he'd drop her off there.

When Mancuso finally pulled up in front of the school at eight twenty-five, he did so in a shiny blue Monte Carlo. I watched as his beautiful daughter, Lisa, got out of the car. From where I was I could see her clearly. As she lifted her legs out of the car her skirt rode all the way up her thighs, and I didn't think it was an accident. I noticed it, and so did some of the boys who were loitering in front of the school. That wasn't enough, though. She had to lean back into the car to kiss her father good-bye, and again her skirt rode up the back of her thighs, even revealing the fact that she was wearing pink panties.

I started to get out of the car to walk over to Mancuso, but he didn't even wait for his daughter to get into the building. He engaged the Monte Carlo and pulled away quickly. I got back into Hacker's Grand Prix and went after him.

I managed to see him make a left at the next corner, which was Rockaway Parkway. I knew he lived on Avenue M between East Ninety-sixth and East Ninety-fifth Streets, so it was possible that he was going straight home. We passed Avenues J, K, and L, and when he approached M, his turn signal did not go on. He passed M, went on by N and then past Seaview, which meant he had to be heading for the Belt Parkway. If he got on the Belt going east, he'd be going to Long Island. If he went west, he'd be going through Brooklyn toward Manhattan.

As he approached the highway, his right signal went on. He was going west. As we went past the Flatbush Avenue exit I wondered how far we were going to go. I got my answer very quickly, because he got off the very next exit, which was Sheepshead Bay.

As I was following him, keeping a lane

and about two or three cars away from him, I wondered if the police knew that Mancuso drove a shiny blue car. He certainly had enough reason to kill his wife, if she was fooling around on him as much as I had heard, but what the hell would he have been doing driving her to the hotel? That just didn't figure at all.

I must have still been half asleep, because it never occurred to me that he might be going where he was going. Even while I was following him down Emmons Avenue it still didn't hit me. He turned his left signal on as we passed Maria's Restaurant, made a U-turn around the island that ran down the center of Emmons Avenue, and then made a right turn into a restaurant parking lot. I stopped my car farther up and watched in the rear-view mirror. He came walking out of the parking lot with a dark-colored attaché case in his hand. The place was closed, but when he knocked on the door it was opened to allow him inside. He smiled, laughed, said something and went inside.

I sat in my car, stunned.

What was Anthony Mancuso doing at Dominick Barracondi's restaurant?

I drove farther down Emmons Avenue, found a pay phone in front of a newsstand,

and dialed the Rectory. When Mrs. Graf answered I said, "Hello, how are you," and asked for Vinnie. She asked me to hold on. She was considerably more pleasant than she had been at first. Flowers can work wonders. It was then I remembered that I was supposed to send flowers to Tina at the hotel. I was just sorry that Giambone was going to get the credit.

"Nick?"

"Quick question, Vinnie," I said. "What does Anthony Mancuso do for a living?"

"Let me think a minute. Um, I think he's — yeah, that's right, he's an accountant."

"An accountant?"

"That's right. Why, what's going on?"

"Did you know that he drove a shiny blue Monte Carlo?"

"No, I didn't."

"Did Gloria have her own car?"

"Yes, she did."

"What kind?"

"A red sports car. I don't know the model."

"So why would she have had to be dropped off at the motel that night?" I asked, talking to myself as much as to him. "And if her husband dropped her off, why? He would have had to know what she was going there for, unless he was totally blind and stupid, and a fool to boot."

"A lot of husbands are," he said. "I can't tell you how many husbands come to me to pour their hearts out about their problems, and they never have an inkling."

"I guess," I said. "Look, I gotta go, but before I do, I just remembered something I wanted to tell you about."

"What's that?"

I told him about my talk the previous morning with Monsignor Genovese, and how I had the distinct impression that the man was very bitter toward Vinnie.

"You know, that's very interesting, Nick," Vinnie said. "Even though he has said that he would back me all the way, he's been very cold toward me. I thought I was imagining it."

"Well, you're not, so watch your back, brother." It seemed odd to have to tell him to watch his back in a Rectory. "Vinnie, what do you know about Father Kelleher?"

"What about him?"

"Did Gloria flirt with him?"

"I imagine so."

"But you never saw them together?"

"What do you mean, together? You don't think that Father Kelleher — Nick, we're talking about a very pious man here."

"Vinnie, I'm just trying to find out if you

were the only priest she came on to, and Father Kelleher is the only other one your age."

"She might have . . . come on to the older ones, too."

"Are you saying —"

"No, I'm not saying she did," he said, "I'm just saying it could have happened."

Sure, I thought, and any one of them could have driven the shiny blue car. My brother was getting worked up, and he had enough on his mind. I decided not to pursue the matter with him any further.

"Did you get those blood-test results yet?"

"No, not yet. I'm waiting for Heck to call. I just hope the detectives don't bring them here in person." He was joking, I knew, but you couldn't have told by the tone of his voice.

"I'll keep in touch, big brother."

"Thanks, Nick."

After I hung up I bought a *Daily News* and a New York *Post* and took them to the car. The *News* headline had to do with a truck hijacking, where a driver had been killed. The *Post* headline had to do with Donald and Ivana Trump. The things that passed for news these days.

I started the car and pointed it toward Bay

Ridge. I needed time to think about the implications of Mancuso's going to Barracondi's restaurant. If he was going on business, that meant that he probably was Nicky Barracuda's accountant.

I didn't like the sound of that.

33

I found a parking spot on Third Avenue, just off Eighty-fourth Street. According to the address Tina had given me, Riley lived on this block, between Eighty-third and Eighty-fourth Streets.

Approaching the building, I realized that I didn't know if Riley was his first or last name. Still, if I had asked her that, even she might have become suspicious.

The address was a Chinese laundry, and next to the laundry was another door. There were two doorbells next to the door, each with a name tag. One said T. HOM and the other said R. HORNSBY. I rang the downstairs bell first, several times. When there was no answer, I rang the upstairs. There was no answer there, either. From the name on the upstairs bell I assumed the occupants were Chinese. That meant that maybe the whole family was working in the laundry.

I went into the laundry and approached the counter. The place had that age-old musty smell of steam and starch. There was a pretty girl there, about sixteen, and an older woman of indeterminate age. She could have been fifty or eighty. She had a mouthful of gold crowns.

Before I could say anything, the older woman said, "You got shirts?"

"Uh, no, no shirts. I want to —"

"You got ticket?"

"No, no ticket." If she said "No tickee, no shirtee," I was going to walk out. I didn't give her a chance. "I'm looking for Riley."

"No Riley," the older woman said, shaking her head. "Shirts or tickets. No Riley." With that she turned and went through a doorway to the back.

The young girl remained where she was, studying me. I smiled.

"Hi," I said. "The whole family work down here?"

"Yes," she said. "Why do you want Riley?"

"I want to talk to him," I said. "Does he live here? Downstairs?"

"Riley and me are friends," she said, twirling her beautiful black hair around her finger. "Good friends. I could give him a message."

I wonder if her mother — or grandmother — knew that she and Riley were "good friends." She was very pretty, with long, straight black hair that probably went down to her ass. She had a round, high-cheekboned face and a body that was full for a sixteen-year-old — especially a Chinese sixteen-year-old. I wondered if she had any sisters. I wondered if Riley liked living here.

"What's your name?"

"Helen."

"Helen," I said, taking out a five-dollar bill, "give him this." I handed her the bill and said, "Tell him it's my calling card."

"This?" she said, raising her eyebrows.

"Just that. He'll know what it means. Thanks."

I left the store and started for my car when I thought of something. If the whole family worked in the store, that meant they'd probably be going up and down from time to time. It'd be a bitch to keep unlocking the door.

I hadn't tried the door the first time, and since I didn't have to pass the laundry to get to it, I went back. I didn't stop at the door and look both ways. That would have been a dead giveaway that I didn't belong there. Instead, I simply grasped the door handle and depressed the lock with my thumb. The door opened, and I stepped in.

I was in a hallway. Ahead of me was a steep flight of stairs, and alongside the stairs was a thin hallway leading to a door. I had to slide past a motorcycle to get to the door. The bike was probably Riley's.

When I reached his door I tried it instead of knocking. It was unlocked, and I opened it. As soon as I did, the smell hit me. It was the brackish, metallic smell of blood, and lots of it. I had smelled it enough times when I was a cop. It was the kind of smell you can taste, the kind that stays with you for days afterward.

I was in a living room and could see off to the side a small kitchenette. I went through the living room to the bedroom, and he was there, on the bed. He'd been killed sometime the night before. I knew that because the sheets had soaked up most of his blood, except for what had coagulated around the neck wound. It was a particularly vicious neck wound, so bad that I thought that when they moved him, they'd better be ready to catch his head when it fell off.

I would liked to have a look around, but I didn't have the time to do so thoroughly. It didn't look as if there had been much of a struggle. Either he'd known his killer, or they had gotten the drop on him.

He was wearing a pair of pants and nothing else. I looked around for his Holiday Inn jacket, but didn't see it. I knew my phone number was somewhere around there, but I didn't want to chance being found there. If the young Chinese girl was right about being friendly with him, then she could be coming back here at any moment. It was bad enough that when the police were called in, she'd be able to describe me as having been there looking for him. Luckily, she couldn't say much more than that.

I went back through the living room and out the front door. Down the hall, past the bike. I got some grease on my shirt. When I reached the front door, I took a deep breath, opened it and stepped out. I headed for my car and didn't look back.

34

I was fitting my key into my door lock when
Sam's door opened. I turned to say something and stopped when I saw her face. Her
left eye and upper cheek were bruised. The
eye was actually puffed and partially closed.

"What the hell —"

"Come inside, Nick," she said. "There's
someone here to see you."

"What the hell happened to your eye?" I
dropped my newspapers on the floor and
walked past her into the apartment. There
was a second surprise waiting for me inside.
Linda Kellogg was there, and if I was any
judge of bruises, the one on the left side of
her face was fresh.

"He did it again?" I said in disbelief.

She nodded, and a tear rolled down her
freshly bruised cheek.

"He would have killed her this time,
Nick," Sam said. "If I hadn't been there, he
would have."

"You?" I said. "What were you doing
there?"

"I knew he was bringing her home from

the hospital," Sam said, "so I went there and followed them home. Nick, they had only just gotten out of the cab when he started hitting her again."

"On the street?"

"I ran across the street to stop him, and he turned and hit me a shot in the face." Sam pointed to her puffed and swollen eye.

"What did you think you were doing?"

"I was keeping that asshole from killing her!" she shot back. "Jesus, her ribs are still taped, for Chrissake!"

"What happened after he hit you?"

"What do you think?" she asked. "I hit him back."

"That must have shocked him."

"It did," Linda said, almost smiling. "God, Nick, she punched him right in the face. She was wonderful!"

"You should have done that to him a long time ago," Sam said.

"And then what happened?"

"Well, I didn't kid myself that I could take him," Sam said, "so while he stood there stunned I kicked him in the nuts." She looked at Linda and said, "You should have done that a long time ago, too." She looked at me again and said, "After that I hustled Linda into my cab and we came here."

"All right," I said, "both of you stay here. I'll be back."

"Where are you going?" Sam asked.

"I think it's time somebody had a serious talk with this asshole."

"Are you going to beat him up?" Linda asked.

"Linda — look, he's hitting my friends now —"

"Nick, please," Linda said, "I love him —"

I nearly blew my top but Sam beat me to it.

"Linda, what are you saying?" she demanded. "The guy's an animal, a serious asshole. He put you in the hospital once, and he would have put you right back there again today."

"If it wasn't for you, I know," Linda said. "Sam, I appreciate what you did; but Nick, I don't want you to hurt him."

"What do you want me to do?"

"I want you to help him."

"*Help* him?"

"Something is seriously wrong, I know it."

"What did he say in the cab on the way home?"

"Nothing," she said. "He had a newspaper and he kept reading it, over and over again, getting angrier and angrier."

"Look," I said, "I'll just go over to your place and talk to him." I doubted I could do that without belting him, but for her sake I was willing to try. Every time I looked at Sam's face, though, I got steamed up all over again.

"He's not home."

"How do you know?"

"I've been calling him. There's no answer."

"Maybe he's just not answering the phone."

"No," she said. "If he's there, he'd have to answer it. It's a phobia with him. He can't not answer a ringing phone. If he's there and not answering, it's because he's passed out drunk. If that's the case, then you won't be able to wake him. He'll have to sleep it off."

I stared at her for a few moments, then said, "All right. I'll talk to him tomorrow. Meanwhile . . . Sam, can she stay here tonight?"

"Of course she can. I'm not gonna send her home so that animal can kill her." She looked at Linda and said, "I'll sleep on the couch, you take my bed."

"It's comfortable," I assured her before she could protest, "I've used it once or twice."

"I don't want to impose —"

"You're not," Sam said.

"I mean, I don't want to get in the way, if you two, uh . . ."

"Oh, no," Sam said, smiling, "Nick and I are friends, Linda."

"Best friends," I said. "No hanky-panky."

Linda laughed and stopped drawing in her breath at the pain her ribs caused her.

"All right, I'll stay."

"And don't make her laugh," I scolded Sam.

"That's okay," Linda said. "It hurts whether I laugh or not."

"Nick," Sam said, "come by in the morning and I'll make breakfast."

"Deal," I said, walking to the door. "You guys don't stay up all night comparing shiners."

As I was leaving, Linda said, "I have nothing to sleep in . . ."

"I have some T-shirts," Sam said, "I always sleep in T-shirts . . ."

I picked up my newspapers and entered my own apartment. I admired Linda's spunk, but had serious doubts about her judgment. I had heard that most battered wives take it and take it and try to hold on to their marriages. I'd seen it on the job, but this was the first example I'd ever seen in someone I knew.

I went into the kitchen and tossed the newspapers on the table. There was some day-old coffee in a pot on the stove and I heated it up. When it was hot I carried a cup to the table and sat down. The back page of the *Post* was facing up, telling me that the Mets had won on a Strawberry homer, but had not gained any ground on the Pirates. They were still two and a half out.

I pushed the *Post* aside and the *News* was face up, still screaming about the truck hijacking. I frowned at it, then opened it to the story and read it. It said that a Mueller Bros. truck had been hijacked, and a driver killed. They said this was the most recent in a long line of recent hijacks.

I got up, walked quickly to my door and pounded on Sam's.

"Who is it?" Sam called.

"Nick."

"What's wrong?" she asked, opening the door. Linda was still on the sofa, but she was wearing one of Sam's T-shirts. This one was pink and said 122ND BELMONT STAKES on it, with a horse and jockey. All the print didn't hide the fact that she had small but firm breasts. Sam was wearing a shirt that simply said BROOKLYN on it. Her breasts were anything but small. Neither of them was wearing anything else but panties. Linda was the only one who tried to hide the fact by pulling the T-shirt down.

"I'm not a Peeping Tom," I assured them. "Linda, what newspaper was Dan reading in the cab?"

"What newspaper? I don't know . . ."

"Think," I said, "was it the *News* or the *Post*?"

"It was the *News*," she said. "He never reads the *Post*."

"All right," I said. "You girls have a job tomorrow."

"What job?" Sam asked.

"I want you to go to the library and look up some old newspapers." I looked at Linda and asked, "Are you up to it?"

"Will it help Danny?" she asked.

"Sweetheart," I said, "it will help all of us."

35

The next morning a pounding on my door woke me up. I immediately remembered that Sam had told me to come over for breakfast, so I assumed I was late. Since I had gotten a flash of Sam's panties the night before, I decided to give her a look at my boxers. In the morning I often work my way up to "playful" before "lucid."

"Okay, sweetcheeks," I said, swinging the door open, "take a good look —"

"Same to you, sweetbuns," Vito Matucci said, slapping me across the face with a folded piece of paper. I caught a glimpse of it and it looked official. I also caught a glimpse of Sam peeking out her door.

"Matucci," I said, "did I invite you for breakfast?"

"If you did, shithead," Matucci said, "I wouldn't be here. You know what this is?" He was talking about the official-looking piece of paper, which he still hadn't held still long enough for me to get a good look at.

"Well," I said, "I only saw it in passing,

but let me guess. Probably the only thing that could bring you up to my penthouse would be a search warrant. How'd I do?"

"Give it to him, Vito," Weinstock said. "Let's get this over with."

"Naw," Vito said, "I wanna make this last."

It was only then that I noticed there was a third man in the hallway.

"You workin' in threes these days, Vito," I asked, "or did they assign someone to teach you manners?"

"Aye," he said, showing me his right index finger. I wasn't impressed. I had one just like it, but a little bigger. Matucci's a bantamweight, and hates it. "I told you, you don't call me by my first name."

"Come on, buddy," I said, "old partners should be able to call each other by their first names."

"Buddy" seemed to bother him even more than his first name, but before he could say anything, the third detective in the hall said, "Can we get on with this? It's crowded out here."

"I'm sorry," I apologized, "I'm being a bad host. Come in."

Matucci took one step forward and I put my hand on his chest to stop him.

"I believe you have a piece of paper for me?"

He frowned and slapped it into my palm. I stepped aside and let them enter. I winked at Sam and closed my door, leaving it ajar. I knew she'd want to listen in.

"Do you mind if I put on a pair of pants?"

"I wouldn't mind if you dropped dead," Matucci said.

"Go ahead," Weinstock said. He was actually a decent guy who had somehow done something to get himself saddled with Matucci as a partner. It had always irked me that Matucci and my father shared the same first name. Weinstock was tall and slender, which was enough of a reason for Matucci to hate him, too. They were both about my age, early thirties or so.

The other detective had already started looking around, which meant he had his mind on business. Matucci had his mind on rubbing my nose in something.

"Who's he?" I asked as Weinstock opened the door to my office and went inside. I probably could have stopped him. I'm sure the search warrant said something about searching my "residence," and the office was my "business" location, but I decided not to be a hard-on about it. There was nothing for them to find in there, anyway. In fact, I couldn't imagine what they would find, but then we're all surprised from time to time.

"Cohen," Matucci said, "six-eight squad. Seems they had a little murder in their precinct, and guess what, shithead? You're on the hot seat."

"Not for murder, I'm not," I said, my mind racing. "That's out of my league."

"Everything's out of your league, scumbag."

"You know, Vito," I said, "more and more you remind me of that detective on 'Hill Street Blues.' You know, the one who bit off some guy's nose, and growls at everybody? He's a shrimp too."

"You son of a —"

"Of course, his language was a little more inventive than yours. After all, that's television."

It was obvious to me by this time that they were here about Riley's death in Bay Ridge. Cohen from the six-eight had probably gone to the CO of my local precinct, the seven-eight, for a local escort, and he'd been blessed with Matucci and Weinstock.

Weinstock came out of my office empty-handed, but Cohen came out of the bathroom carrying something. I recognized it as the shirt I'd been wearing yesterday.

"What'aya got?" Matucci asked.

Cohen held the shirt open so that we

could all see the grease mark across the front. I'd gotten it when I brushed against Riley's bike.

"Found it in the laundry hamper."

Matucci walked up to the shirt and touched it. Then he turned to me, grinning.

"Looks like bike grease to me."

"How would you know?" I asked, my mouth a little dry. "You still haven't out-grown your tricycle."

"You fucker —"

"Never mind," Weinstock said. "Listen, Delvecchio, you were in Bay Ridge yesterday talking to a guy named Riley Hornsby."

"Wrong."

"You deny it?" Matucci asked gleefully.

I spoke directly to Weinstock, ignoring Matucci.

"I went to Bay Ridge yesterday to talk to a guy named Riley Hornsby," I corrected him. "He wasn't home."

"How do you know that?" Cohen asked. He was tall and bulky, older than the rest of us, probably forty-five or thereabouts. Nothing was happening here that he hadn't seen a million times before.

"I rang the bell," I said. "He didn't answer. I'm a detective."

"But you spoke to someone," Cohen said.

He was taking charge. I didn't mind talking to him because he seemed to know what he was doing. I could deal with him. In fact, I even relaxed a bit, even though he was holding a nice piece of evidence in his hand. I sat down on my bed. It's at times like this I wished I smoked. Light one up, blow some smoke rings, be cool . . .

"I talked to two Chinese ladies in the laundry downstairs," I said. "One of them was a pretty thing about sixteen. She told me she and Riley were good friends. I left a message with her."

"Why were you looking for Riley?"

"He's a desk clerk at the Holiday Inn in Staten Island. He was supposed to have some information for me on a client."

"Who's the client?" Matucci asked.

I looked at him and said, "Talk to my lawyer," then looked back at Cohen.

"What's the case?" Cohen asked.

"Runaround wife, using the Holiday Inn for her assignations."

"Assassina—" Matucci said, frowning.

"Trysts," I said, without looking at him.

He made a disgusted sound with his mouth and said, "Keyhole stuff."

I shrugged and said, "Pays the rent."

"Look, Mr. Delvecchio," Cohen said, "I got an ugly murder on my hands. I got a

Chinese girl who's still in hysterics. I got you on the scene, and I got grease on your shirt, which places you inside —"

"I got the grease on my shirt inside the apartment?" I asked.

"There was a motorcycle in the hall," Cohen explained patiently. "You probably got this squeezing by it."

"Can you prove it?" I asked. "You gonna match that grease to one motorcycle?"

"I got enough to haul your ass in now on suspicion," Cohen said, "unless you wanna tell me where you got this grease?"

Sure, I thought, gimme a minute to think.

"Let's take him in," Matucci said. "This asshole ain't got nothin' to —"

The front door opened then and Sam came in, like the Seventh Cavalry — only the Seventh never looked like her.

36

She was fucking with their minds. She had knotted her T-shirt tightly under her breasts, leaving herself bare from there to her pink panties. They didn't know where to look first, her tits, her navel, her thighs . . . I was having the same problem myself.

"Nick, honey," she said, walking right over to me and kissing me. To kiss me she had to bend over and I saw all their eyes go to her ass cheeks in her flimsy panties.

"Oh," she said then, as if just noticing them, "I didn't know you had company. I'm sorry."

"It's . . . all right," Weinstock said, staring at her.

"I just came to get that shirt," she told me.

"What shirt?" I asked.

"Silly," she said, then walked over to Cohen and said, "yeah, that shirt." She took it from his hands before he could react. "Remember? When you dirtied it fixing my car yesterday I promised to wash it for you?"

"Excuse me, miss," Cohen said, finally finding his tongue.

"Yes?"

"He dirtied that shirt fixing your car?"

"He certainly did, the poor dear," she said. "He got all greasy. We had to — I mean, he had to take a shower."

They all caught her "slip" of the tongue, and I know they were thinking about me and Sam in the shower together. So was I.

"I was gonna tell you that just now," I said to Cohen. "All of it except the shower part. I was gonna keep that between my honey and me."

"You're so sweet, Nicky." She came over and stood next to me. They couldn't see her right hand, which was pinching the flesh on my side.

"Where'd you get the shiner, babe?" Matucci asked.

"I beg your pardon?" she said, her tone dripping ice.

"He means, what happened to your face, miss?" Weinstock said, rephrasing it for Matucci.

"Would you believe it?" she asked, touching her face. "I couldn't even open the hood without hitting myself in the face. That's why I needed Nicky."

"Let's take him in, anyway," Matucci

said. "We got enough."

"We got nothing," Cohen said wearily. "He admits being there, he admits talking to the Chinese women, he hasn't lied about anything."

"You say!" Matucci said. "What about prints on the doors?"

"So many people went through those doors before we got there that we got no conclusive prints." Cohen looked at me and Sam and said, "Sorry to have bothered you folks."

"Ain't you gonna ask him if he seen nothin'?" Matucci whined.

"He's a pro," Cohen said, "an ex-cop. If he saw something, he'd tell us."

"Damn straight!" I said.

"Look, you —"

"Weinstock," Cohen said, heading for the door, "bring your partner along."

"Nice of you guys to drop by," I said.

At the door Matucci stopped, said, "Eat shit!" and slammed it.

I stood up, grabbed Sam, hugged her and kissed her soundly on the neck.

"You were fabulous!"

She unknotted the T-shirt so that it fell down, covering her up — sort of.

"Don't you ever call me your honey!" she said, poking me in the chest with her forefinger.

"And don't you call me Nicky."

We stared at each for a few moments, and then I took her in my arms again and hugged her warmly. I was very conscious of her breasts pressing against my chest. We were like that when Linda walked in.

"Oh, sorry —" she said, starting to back out.

"Hey, come back here," I said, releasing Sam reluctantly. "I was just thanking Sam for getting me out of a jam."

Linda was still wearing Sam's T-shirt, and now that she was standing up I could see that she had trim, but firm legs.

"What jam?" Sam asked. "What was that about?"

"The desk clerk from the Holiday Inn? The one I was waiting to call me about some keys? He was killed yesterday."

"Murdered?"

"And then some," I said. "Some son of a bitch almost cut off his head —" I stopped short and looked at Linda, who was gaping at us.

"That's horrible," she said. "Is this another case you're working on?"

"Yes," I said, "My brother's a priest and . . ." I told her the whole story about Vinnie being on the verge of arrest. Maybe I did it to take her mind off her own troubles.

249

"My God," she said, "you've been trying to clear your brother of murder and I've been bothering you with my troubles —"

"Whoa." I walked up to her and took her by her shoulders. "I'm still gonna help you, Linda. Don't worry about that."

"No, no," she said, shaking her head. She had put her hair into a ponytail and it jumped around as she shook her head. Her face washed totally clean of makeup, she looked eighteen, even with the bruises. "I can't ask you to do that. Jesus, your brother needs you —"

"That's enough of that," I said. "You girls have some work to do today, remember?"

"That's right," Sam said. "We'd better get dressed and get to it."

Linda was staring at me with tears forming in her eyes, and then she threw her arms around my waist and hugged me. It would have hurt her ribs too much to throw them around my neck. For the second time in five minutes I had a firm pair of breasts pressing against my chest — smaller, but still firm.

"He's some guy, huh?" Sam asked from close by.

"I don't know what to say," Linda said, her face pressed against my neck.

"Never mind, honey," Sam said, gently

disengaging Linda's arms from around my waist, "let's go get dressed and get to work."

Sam shooed Linda out the door, then turned and gave me a look I couldn't read.

"I'll wash this," she said, still holding the shirt, "so it doesn't get you into any more trouble."

"Thanks."

She nodded and went out, closing the door behind her. Did it bother Sam that Linda had hugged me — and I'd hugged back? Maybe I'd ask her . . . one of these days.

37

I showered and dressed, scolding myself the entire time for throwing the greasy shirt into my hamper, where the cops could find it. I knew they'd found my phone number in Riley's apartment. They hadn't mentioned that, but I knew that's how they had keyed on me. By telling them I was using the clerk on a wayward-wife case, I explained how he happened to have my phone number.

When I got out of the shower I sat with a cup of coffee and tried to figure out how Riley had managed to get himself killed. I'd gone over it last night over a frozen dinner, but my thoughts had been interrupted by a call from Heck Delgado . . .

"Did you talk to Mr. Mancuso?"

I hesitated before answering, then said, "No, he wasn't home." That was the truth. He *wasn't* home, he was at Dominick Barracondi's restaurant. For some reason, I didn't want to mention that to Heck just yet. Not until I checked it out. "Tomorrow's Saturday; I'm hoping to find him home then."

"All right," he said. "Call me at home. I'm very interested in his reaction. Have you found out anything else?"

"Yeah, a few things."

I told him about the clerk seeing Gloria get out of a shiny blue car. I told him that both Mancuso and Vinnie had access to such a car.

"Interesting. Is this the clerk who was supposed to give you the information about the keys?"

"Yeah."

"And did he do that?"

"No."

"Why not?"

"Somebody killed him."

"What?"

I explained about tracking the clerk to his home, and finding him dead.

"It must be related," I said. "It can't be a coincidence. Can you go to the detectives with this?"

"Not without getting both you and Father Vincent in trouble," he said. "You for not reporting it, and Vincent — well, they'll just say that he could have killed the clerk, too."

"Why?"

"Who knows? Maybe the clerk was blackmailing him? Maybe he saw more than just a shiny blue car?"

I thought about that now. It made sense: Riley *had* seen more than just a shiny blue car, and he *had* tried to blackmail someone, and that someone had killed him. It made sense — to me, anyway — that the same person who killed Riley killed Gloria, and tried to pin it on my brother.

I sat up straighter in my chair.

If someone tried to frame my brother for Gloria's murder, and that someone was the one who dropped Gloria off at the hotel, then that meant that Gloria had been in on it. I had that feeling you get when all the puzzle pieces are suddenly dropping into place. If Gloria was in on luring Vinnie out there, then that meant that she was setting him up from the beginning. The only thing she didn't know was that she was setting herself up, as well.

It all made sense to me. The only thing I had to find out now was whom she had been working with. A boyfriend? Her husband? If her husband wanted to kill her, why go through such an elaborate scheme to frame Vinnie? What did he have against Vinnie?

The only one who could shed any light on the subject was Anthony Mancuso himself.

I took about twenty minutes to formulate

the approach I was going to take with Mancuso, then called his house. Its being Saturday was no guarantee that he'd be home, but he had a kid, so it was a good bet he wouldn't be working — especially in light of what had happened to his daughter's mother.

"Hello?"

The voice that answered the phone was that of a young girl.

"May I speak to Mr. Mancuso, please?"

"Who may I say is calling?"

"My name is Nick Delvecchio."

"Delvecchio?" she said, surprised. "That's a priest's name."

"Yes," I said, "Father Delvecchio is my brother."

"Hey, Daddy," she shouted, "Father Delvecchio's brother is on the phone." She didn't bother to place her hand over the receiver.

"Give me that phone," I heard a man say, and then there was the sound of his grabbing it from her. "Go to your room, Lisa."

"But, Daddy —"

"Go ahead, do as I tell you."

There was a pause, and then he came on the line.

"What do you want, you son of a bitch?"

"Hey, Mancuso," I said, "I don't even know you. Where do you get off calling me names?"

"Your brother killed my wife!"

"What's that got to do with me?"

There was a pause and then he said, "Suppose you tell me that. Why are you calling my house?"

"I want to come over and talk to you."

"About what?"

"About the murder of your wife."

"You wanna try and convince me that he didn't do it?" he asked with a sneer in his voice.

"Yeah, I'd like an opportunity to do that."

"Well, fuck off, Delvecchio —"

"Listen to me, Mancuso," I said, cutting him off, "I'm a private investigator working for my brother's attorney, and if you refuse to talk to me, I'm liable to think you're hiding something."

Now there was a pause on his end before he asked, "What have I got to hide?"

"That's a good question," I said. "I'd like to ask it in person."

There was a longer pause and then he said, "All right, come ahead."

"I'll be there in an hour." I hesitated a moment, then said, "Thanks, Mancuso," trying to build up some goodwill.

"Don't thank me," he said. "I may end up kicking your butt right out of here."

38

Mancuso had a big house on a huge lot on Avenue M in Canarsie. There were only two houses on the block, which was a short one. Mancuso's was the larger of the two, with the most land, and a garage. When I got there I pulled right into his driveway. There were parking spots on the street, but I wanted to pressure him right away.

I walked up to his front door and rang his bell. It was answered in moments by Lisa.

She looked at me through the screen door and cocked her head to one side. The way she was dressed — a halter top and cutoff jeans — she looked sixteen, at least. She had her thumbs hooked in the front of the jeans, pulling them down so that I could see her deep navel.

"Are you Father Delvecchio's brother?"

"That's right."

"I didn't know priests had brothers."

"Well, they do. I'm living proof."

"You're not a priest, too?"

"No."

"How come?"

"I guess I just didn't feel I was right for the job."

"Being a priest is a job?"

"I guess they'd say it was more a calling than a job."

"Lisa," Mancuso's voice called from upstairs, "who's at the door?"

She turned her head for a moment, then looked back at me quickly.

"Did Father Delvecchio really kill my mom?"

"I don't think so, honey."

"I hope not," she said as her father came down the stairs behind her, "I really like him."

"Lisa, damn it," her father said, "I told you not to answer the door."

"Well, you were in the bathroom."

"Go to your room."

"Dadd-eee!" she said, drawing it out. "Johnny's coming over."

"I told you I don't want you seeing him. Now go to your room."

"Oooh!" she said, stamping her foot. "You're ruining my life!"

She ran up the stairs and Mancuso unlocked the screen door.

"Damned eighteen-year-olds sniffing around my daughter. She's just a kid."

"She's a beautiful kid," I said. "Maybe

it's got something to do with the way she dresses."

"She's like her mother," he said morosely. "They can smell it on them."

That sounded like a bitter remark directed more at his dead wife than his daughter.

"Smell what on them?"

At that point he just seemed to notice whom he was talking to.

"Never mind! You didn't come here to talk about my daughter." He opened the screen door and said, "Come inside. We'll go into my den."

I entered, he locked the door, and I followed him to the den. We went through an extremely tastefully furnished living room that was primarily light and dark blues. I spotted the dining room, which had a beautiful blond wood table and hutch.

"You have a beautiful home."

"Gloria took care of all the furnishings," he said. "All I did was pay for them."

I followed him into his den, which was spartanly but masculinely furnished. I suspected that he had had more to say about what went in here than Gloria had.

There was a fireplace, and on the mantel was an array of photos. Gloria Mancuso dominated most of them. This was really the first time I had ever seen her, and I could see how men would "smell it" on her. Even in still photographs she reeked of sexuality. It reached out, grabbed you by the throat, and some other parts, as well.

There were a couple of photos of Gloria and Lisa, both laughing. The resemblance was staggering, and looking at the younger girl you could see where she might even surpass the mother, if not in beauty, then in raw sexuality. Unless she went to an all-girls high school, some male students, and teachers, were in for four tough high school years. It was rough having a Lolita in your class.

"She was very beautiful," I said. "I hadn't seen any pictures until now."

"Never mind that." He had seated himself behind his desk. "Say what you have to say. I'm busy."

"You take work home with you?"

"I work at home, Delvecchio," he said. "I'm self-employed . . . and I have some very important clients."

I wondered if he'd get around to bragging. That was one of the things I wanted. I remembered Harriet Dean pushing her little nose over to the side, implying that Mancuso liked to insinuate that he was Mafia-connected. At the time I thought the

261

remark was nonsense, but knowing what I knew now, he might have had connections. Chances were good, though, that he was just an accountant. Nobody with heavier connections than that is going to brag about them to the PTA.

Mancuso looked to be in his late thirties. He was a tall man with broad shoulders and a sallow complexion. He didn't look Italian, he looked more Jewish. His hair was combed straight back, but it was thinning and came to a widow's peak. He was wearing a light-blue short-sleeved button-down shirt, open at the collar. For all the world he looked like the big executive on his day off. That was probably more true of him than "Mafia insider on his day off."

"Important clients, huh?"

"So you know I don't have much time to spend with you."

"What kind of clients?"

He gave me a level stare and said, "The kind you don't want to mess with, son."

"Really?" I said. "Are we talking . . . wise guys?"

"You said it," Mancuso said, "not me. Just believe that I'm not someone you want mad at you."

"Top of the ladder, huh?"

"The very top."

"I guess that explains why you went to Nicky Barracuda's restaurant yesterday, huh? Before it was even open?"

"What?" he said. "What'aya mean?"

"I followed you from school, Tony boy."

"You followed me?"

"So tell me, you do Nicky Barracuda's books?"

"Nobody calls him that anymore."

"Oh, I do," I said. "See, you bullshit people by insinuating that you have these big Mafia connections. I, on the other hand, don't talk about it, but Nicky Barracuda is my godfather."

He sat quiet for a moment, then said, "By godfather, you mean . . ."

"I don't mean Marlon Brando."

"Why are you telling me this?"

"Because I want you to know that you can't shit me, Tony. I'm not in the PTA."

I had him off balance. He knew that he was supposed to be outraged at my presence, since he claimed to believe that my brother killed his wife.

"Now, somebody killed your wife, Tony," I said, "and it wasn't my brother."

"The police think he did it."

"You'll notice that he's not under arrest," I said. "What does that suggest to you?"

"You tell me."

"They have another suspect."

"Who?"

"You know who."

He thought about it for a moment, then said, "Me?"

"Smart man."

"I didn't kill my own wife."

"Convince me."

"I . . . don't have to convince you of anything."

"Okay, then tell me this. If you didn't kill her, and my brother didn't kill her, who did?"

"You didn't know my wife, or you wouldn't have to ask that."

"What do you mean?"

"Men, Mr. Delvecchio." All of a sudden I was "Mister" Delvecchio. "They couldn't stay away from her, and she couldn't keep her hands off of them."

"And you knew this?"

"Yes."

"Why did you stay with her?"

He spread his hands in a helpless gesture and said, "I loved her."

"Enough to be a willing cuckold?"

"Not willing," he said, "helpless."

Jesus, I thought. I hoped I never loved a woman so much that I'd be helpless. Then again, a woman who looked like Gloria

264

Mancuso, who had her . . . particular brand of sexual magnetism . . .

"So you're saying that any one of her boyfriends could have killed her."

"She didn't have boyfriends," he said, "she had men, and she had them once. She never carried on an affair with a man. She had him once, and then came back to me."

"So that's what she was doing at the hotel in Staten Island?" I asked. "Meeting a man?"

"She was meeting your brother. He's admitted as much."

"Yes, I know," I said, "but he didn't stay. He didn't sleep with your wife, Tony. He didn't kill her. He left her alive. He had no motive to kill her."

"If he walked out on her," Mancuso said, "that would have given her a motive to kill him. No man ever turned her down."

"Tony," I said, "did you drive her to the hotel?"

I watched him carefully as I asked the question.

"Drive her?" he asked. "Hell, no, why would I drive her to meet with another man?"

"You've said you were helpless before her."

"Not that helpless," he said. "Believe me,

Delvecchio, I didn't pimp for her. She didn't need a pimp. She was better than any whore at what she did."

The last was said bitterly. I wondered if a man could actually be that helpless, and if so, for how long?

I left Mancuso's house assuring him that I intended to find out who killed his wife. Ever since I told him I was Nick Barracuda's godson he had dropped his superior attitude and adopted one of deference. I guess he figured I had no reason to lie about it.

Outside I started down the walk, but stopped when I saw Lisa waiting for me by my car. She was still wearing the halter top, and she had her hands pushed into her back pockets, which thrust her breasts forward. I had never seen a thirteen-year-old with her degree of development.

"I thought you were in your room?"

"I can't stay in my room," she said. "Johnny's coming to get me."

"But your father —"

"Oh, he won't even notice that I'm gone. He doesn't love me, anyway."

"Why do you say that, Lisa?"

"He says I'm too much like my mother, and he hated her."

"Hated her? But he just told me how much he loved her."

"He lied," she said matter-of-factly. "He's glad she's dead."

"Did he say that?"

"No," she said, "but I've heard him tell her that he wished she was dead plenty of times."

"Well, Lisa, sometimes adults say things they don't mean."

"That's stupid," she said. "People should say what they mean. Take Johnny, for instance. He tells me exactly what he wants."

With a degree of sick fascination I asked, "And what's that?"

"He wants to fuck me," she said, as an old car pulled up in front and the boy behind the wheel beeped his horn.

"Lisa, I don't think that's such a good idea —"

"Oh, don't worry about me, Mr. Delvecchio." She spoke to me over her shoulder as she turned to run to the car. "I'm not a virgin, you know."

No, I didn't know, but watching her run to the car, just thirteen years of firm young flesh, I could believe it.

39

I decided to find out what was going on with Mancuso and Dominick Barracondi, so I drove to Sheepshead Bay. They would probably be setting up for lunch about now.

When I got there I parked in the restaurant's parking lot and walked to the front door. It was unlocked, and I walked right in.

"Hey," a man said, blocking my path, "we ain't open yet."

In the old days he would have been called a torpedo. Here he was probably called a headwaiter.

"Benny around?"

"Who's askin'?"

"Nick Delvecchio."

If he recognized my name, he didn't show it.

"Wait here."

I waited while he disappeared, and a few moments later he reappeared with Benny. Benny said something to the guy, who veered off as Benny approached me. Benny was wearing a charcoal three-piece suit, an orange shirt, a light gray tie, and his pinky rings.

"Hello, Nicky D."

"Benny," I said, nodded. "Is he in?"

"Yeah."

"I'd like to see him."

"I'll have to ask him," Benny said. "Wait here."

"I can do that," I said. "I've had practice."

This time Benny disappeared and when he reappeared he was alone. The torpedo-turned-headwaiter was standing at the bar, and Benny waved to him.

"Come on, Nick."

As I followed Benny, the headwaiter took up his former position by the door.

When I entered Barracondi's office, he was seated behind his desk. I don't know why, but I had the feeling he already knew why I was there. Maybe Mancuso had already called him.

"What can I do for you, Nicholas?"

I sat down, uninvited.

"Tell me about Anthony Mancuso."

"Why should I?"

"Because you're playing games," I said. "You said you wanted to help Father Vinnie, but you were waiting to be asked. All that while you knew that Vinnie was suspected of killing Gloria Mancuso, your accountant's wife."

"What has that got to do with anything?"

"I'll tell you what," I said. "Mancuso's got more motive to kill his wife than Vinnie ever could."

"Maybe he did. I still don't understand —"

"No, I guess you don't, and I don't, either. Who do you want to help, Vinnie, or Tony boy?"

He hesitated a few moments, then said, "Look, Nick, Tony couldn't have killed his wife."

"Why not? Because he's your accountant?"

"Because it's just not in him. He's not a made guy, he's just an accountant."

A "Made Guy" in Mafia parlance is someone who has earned his wings by killing someone.

"Then you better tell him to stop bragging to the PTA about his Mafia connections."

"All right, so he's got a big mouth. That doesn't make him a killer."

"My information is that he hated his wife."

"Still doesn't make him a killer."

"Then you think Vinnie did it?"

He gave me an exasperated look and said,

"Of course I don't think Father Vincent killed her."

"Then give me a name," I said.

"Are you asking for my help?"

"I'm asking you to give me some idea who might have killed her if Vinnie and Tony didn't."

"I can't," he said. "She had too many men. She was an embarrassment to Anthony. If he killed her, I couldn't blame him."

"If he killed her and framed Vinnie, I could blame him for that."

"He couldn't have framed Father Vincent," Barracondi said. "He's not smart enough."

"I think he did it," I said. "If not, then I think he knows who did. He knows *something*. I just came from his house and that's the impression I came away with."

"I can't help you there, Nicholas. I have friends in the Police Department, the DA's office. I can help you there."

I stood up and said, "I don't want you pulling strings to get Vinnie off. I want to prove his innocence."

"Did you ask Father Vincent if he wants my help?"

"I did, and he said no."

"And your father?"

"You know my father. Of course he wants to call you, but Vinnie won't let him."

"If my old friend does call me," Barracondi said, "I will help him."

"He won't call," I said, heading for the door.

"Nicholas!"

I turned.

"You reject my help, you treat me with disrespect —"

"I have *never* treated you with disrespect," I said, interrupting him.

He executed a small bow with just his head and said, "I stand corrected. Let us call it *disdain*. You reject me and treat me with disdain, and yet if you come to me later for help, I will give it."

"Just answer me this," I said. "How connected is Mancuso?"

"He is an accountant."

"Whose?"

"Mine," he said. "He is my accountant for this, my legitimate restaurant. That is all I can tell you. I do not know who else he works for."

"All right," I said, feeling frustrated. I had expected to learn a lot more. "All right . . . if I've treated you with disrespect, I apologize."

"We have determined that what you

have for me is disdain."

"I have disdain for what you represent."

"These days I am a restauranteur, Nicholas," Barracondi said, "and nothing more."

"A restauranteur with strings right up to City Hall, huh?"

"I told you, I am not without influence."

"I'm sure," I said. "I'll be leaving now."

"Come back anytime, Nick, for help, for lunch . . . I would like it if you came back."

"Well," I said, "the food *is* pretty good."

I didn't know what to say further, so I just gave him a half wave and left.

As I left I heard him say, almost to himself, "*Pretty* good?"

Outside I found Benny waiting to escort me out. As we walked to the door I figured, what the hell? Benny had always liked to talk.

"Benny, what do you know about Tony Mancuso?"

"He's a pencil pusher." His tone was noncommittal, but I still managed to notice some — Nicky Barracuda had come up with a good word — *disdain*.

"Connected?"

"What's connected?" Benny said, shrugging. "He works for some guys, keeps their books."

"Like who?"

"Like the Don."

At the door I said, "I know he keeps the Don's books, Benny. I want to know who else's books he keeps."

"Didn't you ask the Don?" Benny asked, opening the door and letting the sun in.

"Yes, I asked the Don, and he said he didn't know."

"Well," Benny the Card said, "if he don't know, I don't know."

I patted him on one broad shoulder and said, "Somehow I knew you'd say that, Benny."

40

I wasn't entirely unhappy with the day's findings, so far. I was convinced that Anthony Mancuso knew something, and I was convinced that Nicky Barracuda knew something. Mancuso was hiding it, Barracuda was simply not sharing it. I was also convinced that I was the only one who *didn't* know something.

So why wasn't I unhappy? Simple. Mancuso knew that Vinnie hadn't killed his wife. Barracuda also knew that Vinnie wasn't guilty. That meant that, eventually, I'd be able to prove that Vinnie was innocent. The proof was out there, I just had to keep looking. I just hoped I'd find it before Vinnie was arrested.

I was driving west on the Belt Parkway, toward Manhattan, trying to figure out my next move, when I noticed I was being squeezed. I hadn't noticed it earlier because I'd been paying only partial attention to my driving. That was the reason I had been driving in the right lane in the first place.

Now I noticed that there was a car directly in front of me, driving slowly, and there was a car riding right next to me. There were two men in each car. We were approaching an exit and they weren't giving me any time to think. The car on my left came over and made contact with me, and the car in front of me slowed almost to a crawl. I had no choice but to go off onto the shoulder. The front car went with me, and stopped, as did the car on my left. It stopped right up against me, pinning the driver's-side door closed. I had one way out, and that was the passenger side. I didn't want to get out, though. At least, not empty-handed. I locked all the doors and started feeling under the seats hoping to find a tire iron, or something . . . anything. All I found were some computer magazines.

By this time the four thugs were banging on the car doors. One of them went to his car, opened the trunk and took out a baseball bat. It looked like a Don Mattingly model. At least they were going to use a best model to cripple me with.

The other three backed away so the one armed with the bat could get a good swing. He hit the driver's-side front window once, and it starred. The second time, it shattered, and then they were reaching in to unlock the door. The next thing I knew I was being dragged out.

There were four of them. I was hopelessly outnumbered and unarmed, but there was one thing they hadn't counted on.

When I was on the job I once had taken a terrible beating because I had been slow to resort to violence. After months in the hospital I swore that I would never take a vicious beating like that again, from anyone. That was the reason I ultimately had to cut a deal to leave the job so as not to go to jail. I had beaten up a guy who turned out to be a politician's son.

Since then I've always carried that fear inside of me. Last year it had caused me to kill one of two men who were bent on giving me a beating.

Now there were four, and as they dragged me out of the car, I exploded in blind fury . . . and fear.

They had me by one arm and both legs. I poked one of them in the eyes, digging in with my nails hard. He screamed and released my other arm. I reached out and grabbed two handfuls of hair, pulling with all my might. Hair came loose in my hand and two more screams sounded. My legs were free and I was rolling away, trying to get to my feet. Before I could I felt the bat hit me in the lower back. The pain was numbing, but I kept rolling and finally got to my feet. My back was on fire then, but the adrenaline flow was keeping me from giving in to it. If I gave in, I'd be on the ground and they would be free to cripple me, or beat me to death. I'd *make* them kill me before I would allow them to cripple me.

The one whose eyes I had clawed was out of it. Blood was running down his face. I hoped I had blinded the bastard for life.

The other three were advancing on me, the one with the bat in the middle. I charged him, and he swung the bat. It hit me on the shoulder, but I ignored the pain. I charged into his midsection and lifted him up off the ground. I carried him a few feet and then slammed him down on his back. When he hit the ground all of the air rushed out of his lungs, and he released the bat and I grabbed it. Giddy with triumph I started to turn and swing the bat, but the other two were on me, and they were big boys. Their weight bore me to the ground, with them on top. I fought like a wild man, but my arm was pinned and the bat was useless. Finally, I let it go so I could use my hands, my nails, but one of them was kneeling on my arm and it was pinned.

"Hold 'im," someone yelled.

"This motherfucker is crazy!" someone else said.

"I got the bat," another voice said. The third man had probably regained his feet. "Hold him. I'm gonna cripple the bastard."

I screamed then, in fear and frustration and just plain anger, and something hit me in the head. The last thing I remembered seeing was Benny the Card's face over the shoulders of my assailants . . . or was that a dream?

When I woke up I knew where I was immediately. I could smell it. I knew what a hospital smelled like, because I had spent almost three months in one back when I had been beaten up. For one stark staring mad moment I thought that I was *still* in the hospital from that beating, and that everything that had happened since then was a drug-induced dream.

"Jesus," I said, out loud, "Jesus, Jesus . . ."

"He's panicking," someone said.

"Oh, Christ," I said, because now I knew I was in the hospital again, and maybe this time I wouldn't get out in one piece.

"Fuck," I said, and then shouted, "Fuck, goddammit!"

"Easy, Nick, easy," someone said, and I felt hands on me, two sets of hands.

I looked to my right and saw Vinnie standing over me. Then I looked to the left and saw Sam.

"Take it easy," she said, smiling and putting her hand on my face, "you're all right."

"God," I said, "am I in one piece?"

"Yes," she said, "you're going to be fine."

"Vinnie?" I said, as if I thought Sam was lying to me. "Vinnie?"

"Nick, you're fine."

"They were gonna cripple me."

"Nick, they didn't . . ."

I didn't believe them. I couldn't feel anything from the waist down, and suddenly I couldn't catch my breath.

"Vinnie . . ." I said, but everything started to spin, and the last thing I heard was someone shouting, "Get the doctor."

The next time I woke up I did so slower, and easier. I frowned, took a deep breath, and recognized the hospital smell. The thing that kept me calm was that I could feel pain in my back. If I could feel pain, then I wasn't paralyzed.

I turned my head to the right and realized that I had a bruiser of a headache. That was good, too. Gimme pain, I thought.

I saw Sam sitting in a chair next to my

bed, and her eyes were closed. I turned my head the other way and saw Maria on the other side, in the same state.

"Jesus," I said, "can't a guy get any attention around here?"

Vinnie was out in the hall or the lounge with Pop, and Maria went to get them. Sam held a plastic cup of water so I could sip from a straw.

"What hospital?" I asked.

"Methodist."

"How long?"

"Today is Sunday. You've been here overnight, and all day."

"Who brought me in?"

"That guy, Benny, who works for your, uh, godfather?"

"Then it wasn't a dream."

"What wasn't?"

"I thought the last thing I saw when I went out was Benny's face. Jesus, my back is killing me . . . and my head . . . and my shoulder . . ."

"That about covers it," Sam said. "What did they hit you with?"

"A baseball bat."

"That's what the doctor said."

"Did he say a Don Mattingly model?"

"Dave Winfield, I think."

"Nobody's perfect."

The door opened and my family came in. Sam touched my arm, the one with the intravenous tube in it, and then moved away from the bed to make room.

"How you doin', little brother?" Vinnie asked.

"Okay," I said, "I think. Did I, uh, freak out . . ."

"That was earlier this morning," Vinnie said. "We explained to the doctor about, uh, the last time, and he thought you might be suffering some flashback. You hyperventilated and passed out."

I turned my head and saw my father.

"Hi, Pop."

His eyes were red, and he hadn't shaved.

"How do you feel?" he asked in a soft voice.

"I'm okay," I said. I felt his hand on my other arm and for a moment I had the urge to cry, but it passed. I guess I was glad to see that he was worried, and relieved.

"What's the damage?" I asked.

"The doctor's going to come in and talk to you about that," Vinnie said, "but there doesn't seem to be anything permanent."

"Good news," I said. "Vinnie, why don't you take Pop and Maria home?"

"I wanna stay," Pop said.

"Me, too," Maria said.

"I want you guys to go home," I said. "You look like you been here all night."

"We have," Vinnie said, "all of us. I could use a shower."

"Go home, Pop," I said, "get some rest, and then come back. I don't think I'll be goin' anywhere for a while."

Pop looked at Vinnie, who nodded.

"You do what-a the doctor tells you," Pop said.

"Scout's honor."

"I never could get-a you to join the scouts," he said, putting his hand on my arm again.

"Come on, Pop," Vinnie said. "I'll see you later, Nick."

Maria came close to the bed so she could kiss me on the cheek.

"See you, big brother. I'm glad you're okay."

"Me, too, sis."

"Sam?" Vinnie said. "Can we give you a ride?"

She was standing off to the side with her arms folded. She was wearing a sundress instead of a T-shirt, and it left her arms and shoulders bare.

"I have my car, thanks. I'll be leaving in a few minutes."

"See you later?"

"I'll be here," she said, and Vinnie touched her arm and started for the door.

"Hey, Vin?"

"Yeah?"

"You're not — I mean, they didn't —"

"I'm not under arrest, if that's what you're trying to ask. No changes, Nick. See you later."

I nodded, and he left. Sam came around to the left side of the bed and took hold of my free hand.

"You scared the shit out of us, pal."

"Scared the shit out of *you?*" I said.

She squeezed my hand and we were silent for a moment.

"While we wait for the doctor," I said, breaking the silence, "why don't you tell me what the fuck is going on?"

41

This part Sam got from Vinnie, who got it from Benny, so I was getting it third-hand. Anyway, it went like this:

After I left Nicky Barracuda's office, he called Benny in and told him to follow me. Vinnie asked Benny why, but Benny said he didn't know, and besides, when the Don tells him to do something, he never asks why.

So, Benny got into his Cadillac and started after me on the Belt Parkway. Vinnie asked Benny how he knew I'd be driving west on the Belt, and Benny told him that's what the Don said. Actually, that wasn't hard to figure. Barracuda knew I had come to his place from Mancuso's home in Canarsie, so I wouldn't have had a reason to go back that way.

Benny was driving pretty fast, trying to catch sight of the car I was driving, when he saw three cars pulled off onto the shoulder. It looked like a bunch of guys beating up one guy.

"Actually," Sam said at this point, "Benny said that it looked like you were beating up on a bunch of guys, but he stopped to help you, anyway. Father Vincent said that it sounded to him like Benny was really impressed with the way you were handling yourself."

"That's because I bugged out."

Benny got there just as I was about to be beaten to death, and he pulled the four guys off me.

"Benny said he routed them," Sam said.

"What?"

She laughed and said, "That was Benny's word."

I laughed, and then cringed because laughing made my head hurt.

"I wish I could have seen that."

"What did you do to them?" Sam asked. "Benny told Father Vincent that you ripped the eyes out of one of them."

"Sam," I said, "I honestly don't know what I did."

"Well, Benny put you in his car and drove you straight here. He then called Mr. Barracuda, who in turn called Father Vincent. Your brother made the other notifications, including calling me. I was the first one here, because your brother stopped to pick up your father and sister, but Benny wouldn't talk to me."

"He wouldn't?"

"Oh, he was very polite," she said. "He called me 'ma'am' and said he would rather wait for the family to arrive."

"Well," I said, "I guess I've Nicky Barracuda and Benny the Card to thank for the fact that I'm not crippled, or dead."

"Does that bother you?"

"I hate to admit it, but no."

At that point the door opened and a doctor entered. He was pretty young, probably about thirty-five, and he had a bright smile for Sam. What man wouldn't? He was not tall, but was athletically built. He had brown hair and a bushy brown mustache.

"Nick, this is Dr. Sconzo. Doctor, your patient." She backed away from the bed to allow the doctor to approach.

"How are you feeling, Mr. Delvecchio?"

"How should I be feeling, Doc?" I asked. "What's the damage?"

"Well, we did some X rays while you were unconscious. You have some definite lower-back trauma, and — excuse me, Miss Karson — you might be passing blood for a while, but there isn't any permanent damage. The same goes for your shoulder. You've got a deep bone bruise there, and it will probably bother you for a while, but there were no broken bones. As for your head, you took fifteen stitches just below the hairline, and you have a slight concussion. You'll probably have a small scar as a memento of this incident. I understand there were four men, and a baseball bat?"

"Don Mattingly model," I said. "It's odd that I should have noticed that."

"In a stressful situation," he said, "our senses are very often heightened."

"When can I get out of here?"

"Well, you *could* walk out of here right now, but I'd prefer to keep you a few days for observation."

"I'll split the difference with you," I said. "I'll check out tomorrow."

"Nick —" Sam said.

"I've got to wrap up both of these cases, Sam," I said, "and I think I know how to do it."

"You're free to check yourself out at any time," the doctor said, "but talk to me first. I want to put that arm in a sling."

"Thanks, Doc."

"You're welcome," he said. He turned to Sam and asked, "May I see you in the hall, Miss Karson?"

"Of course." She looked at me and said, "I'll be right back."

They went out into the hall and I wondered what the doctor could be telling her that he didn't want me to hear.

She was back in a couple of minutes, an amused look on her face.

"What was that about?" I asked. "Am I gonna drop dead in a day or two, and he doesn't want me to know?"

"No, nothing like that," she said. "In fact, it didn't have to do with you at all."

"Oh?"

"He asked me out."

"Oh . . . and what did you say?"

"I said no."

"How come?" I asked. "He's good-looking, and he's a doctor. He must have money."

"Ni-i-ck!" she said, her tone scolding as she drew my name out. "He's also got a wife."

"Oh . . . well, you wouldn't have liked him, anyway."

"Why not?"

"Never mind," I said. "Where's Linda?"

"Probably outside. She said she didn't want to stay at my place alone, and she's not ready to go home."

"Well, tell her to come in."

"I'll go and get her."

She went out of the room and was back in seconds with Linda.

"I'm sorry you had to wait out there," I said, "but I didn't know you were here."

"That's all right," she said. "I didn't want to get in the way, what with your family here and all."

She came to the left side of the bed and surprised me by bending over and kissing me on the cheek.

"How are you?"

"The doctor says I'm gonna live," I said, "but I feel like shit."

"I think I know how you feel."

"Yeah, you would," I said. "How are the ribs?"

"Sore."

"We'll have to compare bruises."

She surprised me again by smiling and saying, "Sounds like fun."

"Never mind the fun," I said, "you ladies had a job to do today — I mean, yesterday. Did you do it?"

"We did," Linda said, looking at Sam.

"The information is at my place," Sam said. "When you come home I'll give it to you."

"All right," I said, feeling groggy. I must have looked groggy, too, because Linda said maybe she'd wait outside for Sam.

"Be well," she said, kissing me again.

"You're quite a hit with the ladies," Sam said.

"Really? Who besides you and Linda?"

"Sister Olivia," Sam said. "You were right, she is pretty. She wasn't wearing her habit."

"When was she here?"

"Earlier today. I don't know if she'll be back." She put her hand on my arm and said, "You should sleep. I'll be outside until Father Vincent comes back."

"You don't have to stay."

"I want to," she said. "Your father was nice enough to say that I was practically family."

"He's right," I said. "Do me a favor, hand me the phone before you leave? I have to make a call."

"To who?"

"Heck Delgado."

"He was here earlier today."

"He was?"

She nodded.

"Now there's a good-looking man," she said enthusiastically, "and he's *not* married."

"Don't tell me that he asked you out, too?"

"No," she said, and then added, "not yet."

"Not yet," I said. "Hand me the phone."

"Here," she said, handing me the receiver, "I'll dial it for you."

After my conversation with Heck I tried to go to sleep, but I couldn't. Things were going click! click! click! in my head as puzzle pieces continued to fall into place. He had given me the main piece, and now all the others were slipping right in where they belonged.

I was so excited by having figured it out that I knew I'd never fall asleep.

Until I did . . .

I heard someone speaking, although it was more of a whisper. I opened my eyes and saw Sister Olivia kneeling next to my bed, her hands clasped together, her lips moving. She was wearing her habit, but she still looked pretty.

"Why'd you have to be a nun?" I asked.

She lifted her head, looked at me and said, "Shut up and go back to sleep. I'm praying for you."

I shut up and went back to sleep.

42

Tuesday morning, at 10 A.M., I presented myself at the law offices of Walter Koenig. I had checked myself out of the hospital Monday afternoon, after Doctor Sconzo had fitted me with a sling. The sling was a good idea, because the slightest movement of my left arm was impossible. There wasn't even pain, because I didn't have the strength to lift it high enough to make it hurt.

Both Sam and Vinnie were at the hospital when I checked out, and they both had cars. We decided that it made sense for Sam to drive me home, since she lived just across the hall. Vinnie said he was going back to the Rectory to wait for Heck to call him about the lab tests. The lab had been closed for the weekend, but this was Monday and the results should be coming in soon.

When we got home Linda was waiting in my apartment and the two women made me sit down on the sofa and insisted on making me lunch. While they did that, I went through the material they had gotten from the library. Now that I had Gloria

Mancuso's murder figured out, Linda Kellogg's problem with her husband Dan began to come together as well.

First, though, I had to keep Vinnie out of jail. Since Linda wasn't anywhere near Dan Kellogg, he could wait.

After lunch I called Koenig's office and made an appointment to see him the next morning at ten. After that I convinced the girls that I wouldn't fall down if left by myself, and after they went back to Sam's apartment, I went to bed. It was only two in the afternoon, but I slept through the night, except for a call I got at 8 P.M.

When the phone rang I tried to reach for it with my injured arm — the left one — but it refused to move, so I grabbed it with my right.

"What?"

"Nick? Vinnie."

"What?"

"Are you awake?"

"What?"

"Nick!"

"*What?*"

"Wake up."

"I'm awake."

"We got the results of the test."

"And?"

"It was inconclusive. My blood type is

type O, universal, so they can't prove it was or wasn't me. It could have been anyone. I'm not under arrest . . . yet."

"That's good, Vinnie."

"Go back to sleep," he said. "You need your rest."

"I was trying to get it."

"I thought you'd want to know."

"I did," I said. "Vinnie?"

"What?"

"I'm gonna wrap this up tomorrow."

"What?"

"Tomorrow," I said. "That's a promise."

"Nick, what are you going to do?"

"I'm gonna go and talk to the son of a bitch who framed you . . ."

So at 10 A.M. I was in Walter Koenig's reception room.

"Mr. Delvecchio to see Mr. Koenig."

His secretary looked at me and said, "Mr. Koenig was called away to court."

"We had an appointment."

"He said he made the arrangements for you," she said. "It's all taken care of. He said you really didn't need to talk to him, anyway."

"You mean he was afraid to talk to me," I said, and added to myself, now that he knew that I knew.

"I beg your pardon?"

"Never mind," I said. "Just tell him that when this is all over, I'll be back for him."

She stared at me and said, "Uh, that sounded like a threat."

I smiled at her and said, "Sweetheart, relay it to him just that way."

Sam refused to let me drive to Attica alone, so instead of taking Hacker's Grand Prix I went in her used, red Nissan Sentra, with her driving. When we got there I made her wait outside the prison while I went in to see the bastard who framed my brother because I wouldn't work for him . . .

43

A month earlier an attorney named Walter Koenig had called me and asked me if I would come to his office. Since I knew that Koenig represented Salvatore Cabretta, I balked. After all, a little over five years ago my testimony as a police officer played a big part in putting Cabretta behind bars. My high "morals" wouldn't let me work for him. However, my morals didn't stop me from going to Koenig's office after he promised me two hundred and fifty dollars just to listen. After all, you can't eat morals.

Koenig's office was on Court Street, a healthy hike from my apartment on Sackett Street. The front door had gold lettering on cherry oak wood that said WALTER KOENIG, ATTORNEY, and I entered without bothering to knock. After I identified myself, his secretary said I could go right in. The other two people in the waiting room didn't like that, but it gave me a feeling of power. I just wished I could do the same thing one time in my doctor's office.

Koenig was behind a cluttered desk that

surprised. For one thing, it was small, and that *and* the fact that it was cluttered did not go along with the impression his painfully neat and clean reception area gave. This room — small, sensibly furnished, and anything but neat — seemed to reflect more of the man than the reception room did, which was, of course, only natural. After all, he spent most of his time here.

I might have liked him for that if I hadn't known he was Sal Cabretta's lawyer.

"Ah, Mr. Delvecchio," Walter Koenig said, rising. "I'm so glad you came."

"I'm not sure I am," I said honestly.

"Perhaps if I wrote you a check . . ."

Not wishing to appear *that* mercenary I said, "You can do that later. Why don't you tell me why you asked me to come here?"

"Please, take a seat."

There was only one to take, a straight-backed wooden chair directly in front of his desk, and I took it.

Koenig was in his mid-forties, a tall, slender, but well-built man with curly brown hair the color of shoe polish. I couldn't help but wonder if he dyed it.

"My client wishes to engage your services."

"By 'client' you mean Sal Cabretta?"

He frowned, as if I was under the impression that he only had one client.

"Yes."

I started to stand and said, "We have nothing further to talk about."

"Oddly enough," he said, "you are correct."

"What?" I asked, stopping midway out of my chair, my knees still bent.

"You see," he said sheepishly, "I know that Mr. Cabretta wishes to hire you, but I haven't the faintest idea why."

"He hasn't told you?" I asked. "His own lawyer?"

"Ah, no, he hasn't."

I straightened up and asked, "Isn't that rather odd?"

"I thought so," he said. "I also told him that I had my own investigators. He was quite adamant that he wanted you."

"Why?"

"Alas, I can't answer that," he said. "I've been instructed to pay you for consulting with me, and to ask you to go and see him."

"In prison?"

"Yes."

"I don't understand."

"I have been frank. I don't, either. I'm rather anxious for you to see him so that *I* can find out what's going on."

"I put him away," I said. "At least, my

testimony did. It's ludicrous to think that I'd go up and see him."

Koenig smiled and said, "But it's a fascinating prospect, isn't it?"

He was right, it was fascinating.

"All right, I'll go."

"I'll write your check."

"Double it."

"What?"

"You want me to go to Attica, Counselor, you're going to have to pay my way. Take it or leave it."

He took it.

He pulled a checkbook from his desk drawer, wrote me a check for five hundred dollars, tore it loose, and handed it to me.

"I suppose you'll clear the way for this visit?"

"I'll make some calls, yes."

I stared at him and then said, "You've already made them, haven't you?"

He smiled and said, "How did you guess?"

"I didn't," I said. "I know it, just by looking at you."

"You are a very good detective."

"You're damned right I am," I said. "Just ask your client."

I wasn't a detective when I put Cabretta away, just a patrolman who happened to be in the right place at the right time, but I wasn't about to let that spoil a good exit line.

Sal Cabretta looked every bit as dangerous in prison as he had looked out. The fact that he was wearing prison-issue clothes diminished his stature not one iota. He sat in his plastic chair as if he were sitting in a leather chair behind an oak desk in his luxurious home on Long Island.

"Nick," he said when I walked in.

"I thought I told you a long time ago never to call me that."

Cabretta smiled contemptuously.

"What are you going to do," he asked, "send me to prison?"

I gave way to a small smile and said, "You have a point."

Even here Cabretta was entitled to certain privileges, such as a private meeting room on demand — one that was usually reserved for lawyer/client relationships. I was a private detective, not a lawyer, and Cabretta was certainly not a client. On the contrary, five years ago I had been a cop, and Cabretta was behind bars with my compliments.

That made Cabretta's "summons" even more curious.

"Have a seat," Cabretta said, "I have something I want to talk to you about."

"What makes you think I'm interested in anything you'd have to say to me?"

Cabretta, a good-looking man in his late forties, smiled and said, "The fact that you're here answers that question."

"I'm here because I was paid five hundred dollars to come."

"Five?" Cabretta said, showing mild surprise. "I told my lawyer to offer you two fifty."

"He did," I said, and left it at that.

"I see," Cabretta said. "Will you have that seat?"

I hesitated, then said, "Why not?" and sat across the table from the ex–drug king turned prisoner.

Cabretta turned to the guard who was standing inside the door and said, "Get lost."

"I can't —"

"Beat it, screw!"

The guard looked at me and I said, "It's all right."

"I'll be right outside."

"Stay away from the door!" Cabretta called after the guard as he left. "Fuckin' walls have the biggest ears you ever saw in here," he said. "All right, then, let's get to

302

it. I want to hire you."

"That's a laugh."

"Nevertheless," Cabretta said, "it's true."

Warily, I asked, "To do what?"

"Since I've been here my wife has either visited me or written to me at least once a week, sometimes one of each a week."

"So? She's a faithful wife."

Cabretta frowned and said, "That's what I want you to find out."

"Why?"

"I haven't seen her or heard from her in a month."

"Maybe she's sick."

"I don't think so. I think there's something else going on, and I want you to find out what."

"Why not have one of your goons outside do the job?" I asked.

"Because I want it done in the qt," Cabretta said, "and I don't trust anyone else to do it but you."

"Why's that?"

"You put me here," Cabretta said, "that means you're good at what you do. I want to hire the best."

"I'm good, but I'm not the best."

"I'll take my chances with you, Nick."

"I told you —"

Cabretta raised his hand to stay the objection and said, "Sorry . . . *Mister* Delvecchio."

"Let me get this straight," I said. "You want me to find out why your wife hasn't written or come to see you in a month."

"That's right."

"And then what?"

"And then come back here and tell me."

"You don't want me to report to your attorney?"

"He doesn't know why I'm seeing you today."

"You haven't told your attorney?" I asked in surprise.

"I told you," Cabretta said, "I don't trust anyone on this but you."

I studied Cabretta for a few long moments. His dark hair had begun to show some gray while he'd been inside, but he looked as if he were still keeping himself in shape. He looked fit, with the build of a man ten years his junior.

"Why should I do this for you?"

"I knew you'd ask me that," Cabretta said. "You owe me."

I snorted and said, "For what?"

"For putting me here," Cabretta said, showing the first signs of agitation. "For taking away five years of my life, that's why!"

"You deserve to be in here, Cabretta," I replied casually. "You *belong* in here, and for a lot longer than five years."

Cabretta stiffened his jaw and for a moment I thought he was going to explode. I watched as the man brought his fabled temper under control, and thought that at least he had learned something during his stay here.

"All right," Cabretta finally said, "name your fee, then. You work for people for money, right? Well, I've got money. Name your price."

My regular price was two hundred and fifty dollars a day plus expenses. Things had been rough during the past year, and at times the price had come down as low as *one* hundred and fifty.

"Three hundred and fifty a day, plus expenses."

Cabretta never blinked.

"Take the case and I'll have my attorney pay you a week's retainer."

"And if I don't catch her doing anything . . . wrong during that time?"

"Come and tell me, and then we're quits."

"And if I find that she's seeing someone?"

"Same thing."

"And then she ends up dead? Thanks, but no thanks, Sal."

Cabretta looked appalled and said, "My own wife? And even if she wasn't my wife, I don't do business that way. You know that, Ni— Delvecchio."

He was right, he didn't do business that way. He was a businessman — or a hood in businessman's clothing, but he operated his drug empire in Brooklyn just like any CEO would run his business.

I still wasn't about to go to work for him.

I stood up, walked to the door and banged my fist on it.

"Well, what's your answer?" Cabretta asked.

I turned and said, "Me walking out the door is my answer, Sallie."

At that he stood up quickly, knocking his chair over. His face turned red with anger. At the time something bothered me about his reaction, but I didn't dwell on it then.

"You ain't turning me down, Delvecchio!"

"Watch me," I said, as the door opened.

"You think because you're Dominick Barracondi's godkid you can turn your back on me? That's the reason you *should* work for me!"

I didn't understand that, but I wasn't about to turn around and ask him to explain it to me — and I didn't need to be reminded that *my* godfather was also *the* godfather of Brooklyn.

"You'll be back, kid," he shouted as I walked down the hall. "You'll be back." And then he started laughing. His laughter followed me all the way down the hall, echoing, bouncing off the walls . . .

44

Now I was back in that same room with Cabretta, and he lookcd as if he had never left his plastic chair, like he was waiting for me there all this time, knowing I'd come back.

"You son of a bitch," I said, from the door.

"Walter said you wouldn't figure it out," Salvatore Cabretta said, "but I knew you would. I had confidence in you."

"You low-life scumbag. Once I found out that Koenig was Mancuso's lawyer, it all sort of fell into place. Koenig was the link. He'd never represent a lightweight like Mancuso, not unless you told him to."

He smiled at me.

"Sit down, Nick, and let's talk deal."

"What kind of deal?"

"I can get your brother off the hook."

"He's not on the hook."

"I can do that, too."

"What are you talking about?" I said. "All you've done is heap a bunch of circumstantial evidence against him."

"All I've done so far," he said, "is damage his reputation. There's still one piece of evidence that hasn't been produced yet."

"What's that?"

"You better hope you never have to find out," Cabretta said. "Just believe this, Delvecchio, I can hang him, or I can get him off the hook. It's up to you."

"I can't believe this, Sal," I said. I finally decided to sit down, but only because my lower back was starting to hurt. When I took a piss that morning it had come out red. Luckily, the doctor had warned me about that.

"Is the job still the same?"

"Yes," Cabretta said. "Find out why my wife hasn't come to see me."

I shook my head, not negatively, but in disbelief.

"So to get me to take this job you killed an innocent woman and framed my brother for it."

Cabretta smiled at me and said, "I know you, Nick. You're not wired, so I'm gonna answer your question."

"What makes you think I'm not wired?"

"You'd never have gotten it past the guards."

"Okay," I said, "go ahead and answer my question."

"First of all, I didn't kill anyone. Second of all, Gloria Mancuso was far from innocent. She was an embarrassment to him, and to the family." I knew he wasn't talking about the Mancuso family. "She was a pincushion, Nick. A beautiful pincushion. She'd spread her legs for anything in pants . . . once."

"That include you?"

"Yeah," Cabretta said, "I had her once."

"So Mancuso's your accountant too, huh? And you fucked his wife behind his back."

"No," Cabretta said, "not behind his back."

"He knew about it?"

"What was he gonna do?" Cabretta asked. "Like you said, he's a lightweight . . . a lightweight whose dream it was to be a made guy."

"Are you telling me that Tony Mancuso killed his own wife?"

Cabretta missed a beat and then said, "I didn't say that."

No, but that's what he meant. He'd let something slip, and he wasn't happy about it. I decided to be willing to be convinced.

"What did you mean?"

"All I meant was that the man had a beautiful wife and couldn't satisfy her. There's no one man alive who could."

I studied Sal Cabretta for a long moment and things went click! click! click! Cabretta had always been a ladies' man. How would he have reacted to a woman like Gloria Mancuso? Especially if she had slept with him once and wouldn't repeat the performance? A man like Cabretta wouldn't take that lightly. Would that be enough to kill her? For an egomaniac like Sal Cabretta, sure, but add to that the fact that she was his accountant's wife, and knew some things about his businesses . . .

Click! Click! Click!

What a coup it would be for Cabretta to force Mancuso to kill his own wife, and then pin it on my brother.

But when that was done, why let Vinnie off the hook, just to get me to follow his wife?

Think about it.

Click!

Click!

Click!

Pieces falling into place.

I told Cabretta I'd take his job, but I wanted Vinnie off the hook, *and* I wanted my fee. He agreed, and said that he'd clear my brother when I reported to him about his wife.

I agreed.

He told me I could get all the information I needed on his wife from Koenig.

Just before I left he said, "Welcome to the payroll, Nick."

After I left the prison, before I met with Sam, I found a phone and called Dominick Barracondi. I got Benny, thanked him for what he did, and asked to speak to the Don.

When he came on he said, "Nicholas."

I said, "I need a favor."

45

When I got back to Brooklyn I had Sam drive right to Walter Koenig's office. She waited outside while I went up and presented myself to his secretary again.

"I don't have an appointment this time."

"Yes, you do," she said. "Go right in."

I went into Koenig's office and sat in his visitor's chair. There was a brown 10-by-13 manila envelope on my side of his desk.

"Everything you need to know about Carla Cabretta is in there," he said. "Where she has her hair done, where she has her car serviced, where her health club is —"

"The only thing we don't know," I said, sliding her photo out of the envelope, "is who's fucking her."

"If she is having an affair," he said stiffly. "That is up to you to find out."

I studied the color photo. It looked a studio print, just a head shot — but what a head. If the colors were to be believed her hair was chestnut, her eyes green. She was a beautiful woman, but her photo didn't have the impact of Gloria Mancuso's photo.

There was a second picture, a candid shot of her leaving some place, wearing a leotard. From the looks of her she was tall, with long legs, a tiny waist, small, firm breasts, and wide shoulders.

"Classy-looking," I said.

"Yes, she is."

"All right, Walter," I said, using his first name to his dismay. "I'll get right on it."

"Yes," he said, "you do that." He couldn't wait for me to leave. Now that I was working for Sal Cabretta, he couldn't waste his time on me. I was just another employee.

At the door I turned and said, "Oh, Walter . . ."

"Yes?"

"I assume Mancuso called you after I left his house, and you sent those four goons after me. That right?"

He hesitated.

"Come on, Wally," I said, "we're on the same team now."

He blanched when I called him Wally.

"That was just business," he finally said.

"Sure," I said, "just business. No hard feelings."

There were plenty of hard feelings, but he wouldn't find out about them until later.

Actually, I had asked Dominick

314

Barracondi for more than one favor.

When we got back to my apartment Sam made coffee while I outlined the whole thing for her, including my plan.

"That's devious," she said afterward. "In fact, it's mean."

"I know," I said. We were in the kitchen, at the table, and I said, "Hand me that phone, will you? And then go check on Linda. Make sure she doesn't go back home until I say so, okay?"

"Okay, but I still don't know what you're going to do about her husband."

"I'll tell you," I said, dialing the phone number that was on the back of Carla Cabretta's photos, "after I get this other thing straightened out."

Sam turned one of the photos around and said, "Ooh, classy dame."

"Dame?" I said. She stuck out her tongue at me and left.

Carla answered the phone on the first ring.

"Mrs. Cabretta," I said, "this is Nick Delvecchio."

"Yes, Mr. Delvecchio," she said. "Dominick Barracondi said you would be calling."

"Are you willing to meet with me?"

"I have great respect for Don Dominick,"

she said. "He tells me you have something to discuss with me that is very important."

"That's true."

"What could that be?"

"Your life, Mrs. Cabretta," I said. "Your life."

Carla Cabretta agreed to meet me in Brooklyn Heights, on the Promenade, a small park that hung over the Brooklyn–Queens Expressway. From it you could look across the East River at the classic Manhattan skyline. The Promenade also boasted the hot-dog vendor with the best hot dogs outside of Nathan's on Coney Island.

I was sitting on a bench when she arrived. I had told her how to recognize me. I knew the sling on my arm and the bandage on my head would come in handy.

She walked to me with a long, athletic, purposeful stride.

"Mr. Delvecchio?" she asked.

"Mrs. Cabretta."

"Did my husband have that done to you?"

"Sort of," I said. "Walter Koenig actually gave the order."

"That figures," she said. "Aren't you the police officer whose testimony sent my husband to prison?"

"I am — or was. I'm not a cop now, I'm a private investigator. Please, Mrs. Cabretta," I said, "sit down. What I have to say might surprise you."

She sat next to me, and I got a strong whiff of her perfume. It was a very nice scent. Up close I could see that she looked older than her pictures. From the photos I had made her thirty-five. Now I could see she was probably forty or more, but wearing it very well. She kept herself in shape, this one.

"Well, Mr. Delvecchio?" she said. "If you've finished checking out the merchandise, I'd like to know why I'm here."

"Mrs. Cabretta —"

"Stop calling me that," she said. "If you must call me something, call me Carla."

"Carla, your husband has hired me to follow you and find out why you haven't come to see him in months."

"Why would he do that?" she asked. "He knows why I haven't come to see him. I want a divorce."

"You told him that?"

"The last time I saw him. I told him I wouldn't be back, either."

"Do you have a lawyer?"

"No," she said, "Sal said that Walter would take care of everything. So tell me,

Mr. Delvecchio, why would he send you to follow me to find out something he already knows?"

My answer made even more sense now than it had before.

"Carla," I said, "I'm pretty sure that Sal plans to have you killed, and frame me for it."

She stared at me for a few moments, then said, "That doesn't surprise me, Nick. Can I call you Nick?"

"Sure."

"It worries me, of course, Nick, but it doesn't surprise me," she said. "It also makes sense to me."

"Good," I said. "I thought I was going to have to convince you."

"You don't have to convince me," she said, "but I would like you to tell me what we can do about it."

"I have a plan."

She smiled and said, "I hoped you would."

"Why don't you go and get us a couple of hot dogs, Carla," I suggested, "and I'll tell you all about it."

46

Back to Walter Koenig's office early the next morning. This time I had company in the person of Carla Cabretta and three friends. When I had outlined my plan to her she had reacted much the way Sam had.

"That's mean," she'd said, and then added, "and delicious."

The word "delicious" sounded entirely natural coming out of her mouth.

"It's barely nine," his secretary said to the five of us accusingly.

"That's all right," I said. "Just tell him I'm here, and you won't have to do anything. We won't need you. We can get our own coffee."

"I don't get cof— just a minute. I'll announce you."

"Why don't you go out and get a doughnut or something, honey?" I said, picking up her purse and holding it out to her. "We'll announce ourselves."

She looked at all of us, then took her bag and walked out the door.

"Loyalty," I said, shrugging.

I looked at Carla and said, "Wait here."

"Right."

I went into Koenig's office and left the door ajar.

"What are you doing here?" Koenig demanded. "Where's my secretary?"

"She said something about getting a doughnut."

"I have an early court date, Mr. Delvecchio," he said briskly. He was busy shoving some papers into an attaché case. It looked like an eelskin case, much more expensive than Tony Mancuso's case. Thinking of Mancuso made me look at my watch. "What did you forget yesterday?"

"I didn't forget anything, Walter," I said. "The job's done."

He stiffened, stopped what he was doing and looked at me.

"What?"

"I said the job's done," I said. "I know who's been porking Mrs. Cabretta."

"You know . . ." He stopped and frowned. "Who?"

I smiled at him and said, "You."

He looked stunned.

"That's ridiculous, I've never laid a hand on Carla. What are you trying to pull?"

"What do you think Sal will say when I give him my report, Walter?"

He developed a nervous tick. His mouth kept twitching as if it wanted to smile, but couldn't find anything to smile about.

"You wouldn't — he would never believe you."

"I have a witness."

"A . . . witness? How could you have a witness? I've never touched her, I tell you."

Only someone who was telling God's honest truth could be that indignant, but it didn't matter that he was telling the truth.

"An unimpeachable witness."

"That's not possible," he said. "Who could this witness be?"

I smiled, walked to the door and opened it. Carla Cabretta walked in and smiled at Koenig. I left the door ajar again.

"I'm sorry, darling," she said, "he beat it out of me."

He gaped at her, then at me, and then understanding dawned in his eyes.

"You're framing me."

"Why not? Cabretta had my brother framed for Gloria Mancuso, and he was going to have me framed for the murder of his own wife. I'd say turnabout is very definitely fair play in this case, Walter, wouldn't you?"

"But . . . but if you tell him that, he'll have me killed."

He looked at Carla for support and she said, "I'll shed a lover's tears at the funeral, darling."

"You can't —" he said to her; then he looked at me and said, "You can't —"

"Don't worry, Walter," I said, "I'm a reasonable man. We can work something out."

He stared at us for a few moments, and then sighed and said, "What do you want me to do?"

When the phone rang it was almost six o'clock. When Koenig answered the phone, he knew exactly what to say. He put the call on the speaker box so we could all hear it. I also wanted Mancuso to hear that he was on the box.

"Walter? It's Anthony. What are you doing to me, Walter?"

"I don't know what you mean, Anthony."

"Someone tried to kill me tonight."

"That's impossible, Anthony —"

"What'aya mean, impossible? I know when somebody's shooting at me! You gotta tell Sal I won't talk, Walter."

"Anthony," Koenig said, looking at me, "if someone is trying to kill you, we have nothing to do with it."

"What? You gotta help me!"

"Maybe you got someone mad at you, Anthony."

"Mad at me? Why should Sal be mad at me? I did what he wanted. Jesus, Walter, *I killed my own wife!*"

I looked at Carla Cabretta and she nodded. She was a witness to Anthony Mancuso's unsolicited confession.

I looked at Koenig, mouthed "Wait," made some noises I was sure Mancuso would hear over the box, and then waved at Koenig to go ahead.

"Look, Anthony," Koenig said slowly, "tell me where you are and I'll send someone to get you."

Now there was a pause at the other end and then Mancuso said, "You'll send someone to kill me, you mean! Jesus, Walter — you got men there now, right? You got me on the damned speaker? Walter, I'm going to Nick Delvecchio. You know him? The priest's brother? He's a private detective. He'll know what to do."

I wasn't sure whether he'd come to me or Barracondi, but I was happy he chose me.

I cued Koenig and he said, "Don't do that, Walter. Look, I'll send someone right over to your house —"

"Fuck you, Walter!" Mancuso screamed. "And fuck Cabretta! I ain't gonna be at my house, Walter. I'm gonna put you both away, you bastards!"

"Anthony, don't —" Koenig started, but Mancuso hung up. Koenig shrugged helplessly and turned off the box.

"Now what?" he asked.

"Now I'd like you to meet a few friends of mine." I walked to the door, opened it and waved my three friends in.

"See this fella here? His name is Detective Weinstock. This well-dressed devil over here is Detective Lacy, from Staten Island. He wants to talk to you about Gloria Mancuso's murder. And this other handsome devil is Detective Cohen. He wants to talk to you about a murder in Bay Ridge." I gave Koenig a tight smile as pain coursed through my arm, shoulder, and lower back and said, "Payback's a bitch, Wally . . . fuckin' A!"

I took Carla's arm and eased her toward the door.

"Now don't fight over him, gents."

"Where are you going?" Weinstock asked.

"When you've settled your jurisdictional disputes, we'll be ready to make statements. Meanwhile, I've got to go home and wait for a call from Anthony Mancuso. When I get it, I'll call Weinstock and let you boys know where you can pick him up." Weinstock was the big reason the other two were there. I had convinced him to accompany me, and he had in turn convinced them. I owed him, which might be why he had done it.

"Delvecchio —" Weinstock started.

"Don't thank me, fellas," I said. "Uh, Detective Lacy, would you like me to notify my brother's attorney that he's no longer a suspect?"

Lacy was fitting the cuffs onto Koenig's wrists.

"Mr. Delvecchio," he said, "you can have that pleasure — unofficially, of course."

"Of course," I said.

On the street Carla Cabretta said, "I'm very impressed, Nick . . . and grateful."

"I was just clearing my brother, Carla," I said, "but you know what? I don't think you'll have the slightest problem getting a divorce now. In fact, with the extra time this will add to your husband's sentence, you might even be able to get an annulment from the Catholic Church. Hell, I may even be able to help you with that!"

Epilogue

Two days later I explained everything to Father Vinnie and Sam. I had a choice of where to do the explaining. I could have done it at my father's house, but I decided against it. I also could have done it at the Rectory, but on second thought, that didn't seem like the place to do it. Besides, Sam wanted to hear it, too, so we finally gathered just the three of us — at my place, over a take-out pizza and some beer. Yes, priests eat pizza and drink beer — especially my brother, who liked beer, but loved pizza.

He also was not quite ready to wrap up his own case yet. He was still trying to deal with the fact that he was free of all suspicion.

"Before we discuss my case," Vinnie said, "what happened with that woman you were trying to help? What was her name?"

"Linda Kellogg," Sam said.

"Sam helped me with that," I said, "and so did Linda."

"All we did was go to the library." Sam was being modest. They spent *hours* in the library.

"The library?" Vinnie asked. "What for?"

"Newspaper clippings," I said. "They brought me clippings of stories about recent truck hijackings. As it turns out, Dan Kellogg was beating his wife the day after a hijacking."

"What did that tell you?" My brother's a great priest, but a lousy detective.

"Kellogg was a dispatcher for Mueller Trucking, Vinnie. Some of the hijacked trucks were from Mueller."

"He was setting up hijackings inside his own company?" Vinnie asked, looking shocked.

"Outside his company, too," I said. "He was in touch with other dispatchers from other companies, and pumped them for information, as well. Of course, they never suspected what he was doing."

"But why beat his own wife?"

"She was there," I said, "and he had a lot of anger inside of him. He had to take it out on someone."

"He could have gone to church," Vinnie said, "and talked to a priest."

"Well," I said, "now he's talking to the cops. He's going to cooperate and help them catch the hijackers."

"What will that do for him?"

"He'll make a deal with the DA for a reduced sentence, or maybe even probation.

He *was* being threatened."

"How?"

"Here's the ironic part," I said. "They threatened to hurt Linda."

"So he goes along with them and instead, *he* hurts his own wife?"

I gave Father Vinnie a helpless look and said, "I can't figure it, Vin."

"There must be more to it than that," Sam said.

"If there was," I said, "he'll tell the cops, eventually."

"What about the wife? Linda? What happens to her?" Vinnie asked.

"She loves him," Sam said, "so she's standing by him."

"She's a brave girl," Vinnie said.

"Stupid," I said.

"Nick!"

"Look at it, Vinnie," I said. "Even if he gets off, he's a walking time bomb. The next time he gets angry enough, he could kill her."

"Have you told her that?"

"I did, on the phone."

"And?"

"She hung up on me."

"You did the best you could, Nick," Sam said. "We all tried to help her, but she just can't see life without a husband."

"Then she should find herself another one."

We fell silent and indulged in pizza and beer for a while — more beer than pizza for me. I had lost my appetite. I was dealing with the fact that there were some real similarities between the Kelloggs and the Mancusos. Of course, in the case of Anthony and Gloria Mancuso, it was actually the wife who was abusing the husband until he couldn't take it anymore, while it was Dan Kellogg who was physically abusing Linda. In both cases, though, the wife ended up the real victim — and it could still get worse for Linda. I just hoped that she wouldn't ultimately end up like Gloria Mancuso.

Finally, Vinnie decided it was time to exorcise the last of his own demons. He wanted to talk about his own case. First, I had to explain what would make a man like Sal Cabretta want to frame a priest for murder. I took the blame for that, but he wouldn't have any of it.

"You did the right thing, Nick." His tone was reassuring. "You put a criminal behind bars. You are not responsible for the form his attempt at revenge took."

"He also wanted to kill his wife," Sam said, and we both looked at her. She continued, ticking them off on her fingers. "Three marriages — Kellogg, Mancuso, Cabretta — and three abused spouses."

"And violence the final result," Vinnie said, shaking his head. "What's happened to the once holy state of matrimony?"

"Don't go sour on me, Father Vinnie," I said. "There are a lot of good marriages in the world. We just happened to run across three bad ones."

"You're right," he said. "That doesn't make them all bad."

"Was Cabretta's wife cheating on him?" Sam asked.

"Maybe," I said, "probably. He was convinced she was, though."

"And that was enough of a reason to want to kill her?" Vinnie asked.

"Maybe that was just another way to get back at me," I said, "to kill her and make it look like I did it."

"This is all . . . beyond me," my poor brother said.

"You want to hear the rest of it?"

He stared at me for a moment, and then said, "Yes, I suppose I'd better. Tell me what happened after you left Walter Koenig's office that day." He gripped a bottle of St. Pauli Girl very tightly as he waited for my answer.

"I came back here and waited for Anthony Mancuso to call."

"And he did?"

"Yep."

"And?"

"I told him to come right over."

"And did he?"

"He did."

"What finally made up his mind?"

"I arranged for him to think that Cabretta was trying to have him killed."

"How did you do that?"

The last thing I wanted to tell Vinnie was that I called Dominick Barracondi and asked to borrow Benny, so I said, "I just got someone to take a couple of shots at him."

"Nick, you didn't."

"Oh, the shots missed, Vinnie," I said. "They were just supposed to scare him."

"And they did."

"They sure did," I said, "right into my arms."

"And what did you do?"

"I gave him a sympathetic ear."

"Whose?" Sam asked.

"Weinstock's. He was waiting here when Mancuso got here."

"Your old partner's partner?" Vinnie asked.

"That's right."

"Why him?"

"Because I'd shoot Mancuso before I'd give him to Matucci."

"Matucci's going to hate you even more for this," Vinnie said. "First you give Koenig to Weinstock, and then Mancuso."

"And, extending the arm a little further," Sam said, "Cabretta."

"Yeah," I said, smiling, "Vito's probably mad enough to sh— uh, spit, but I don't think he *could* hate me any more than he normally does."

"So what happens to Mancuso?" Vinnie asked.

"He makes a deal with the DA and gives them Cabretta on a conspiracy-to-commit-murder rap."

"He won't get off," Sam said, staring at me over a wilting slice of pizza, "I mean, surely he can't . . ."

"No," I said, "he won't get off. He'll get life in some country club rather than in a hell hole, but he'll get life."

"But . . . did Anthony Mancuso really kill his own wife?" Vinnie asked in disbelief.

"I'm afraid so, Vinnie," I said.

"That's . . . unthinkable!"

"You've never been married," Sam said, and I stared at her. The way she said it made me wonder if *she'd* ever been married and had never told me about it.

"But still . . ."

"Look, Vinnie," I said, "she was a slut and he was her cuckold. Besides, he wanted to be in the 'family,' he wanted to be a made guy. Cabretta gave him the chance."

"By killing his own wife?"

"Let's not forget," I said, "that he was afraid of Cabretta."

"But why would Cabretta want Gloria Mancuso dead?"

"Gloria wasn't a person to him," I explained, "she was a means to get his revenge on me, to first make me suffer — through *you,* Vin — to then get me to take his case, and then ultimately to have me killed. Put it all together and you've got a motive for murder."

"Terrible," my brother the priest said, shaking his head.

"Hey, that ain't the sick part," I said. "Tony boy screwed her that night."

"Before or after?" Sam asked, and Vinnie gave her a look that asked how she could even ask the question out loud.

"I don't know," I said, "and I don't care."

"And what happens to Lisa Mancuso?" Vinnie asked.

I shrugged. At the mention of her name I remembered her the way she looked the last time I saw her, running toward "Johnny's" car, cutoff jeans riding up her ass cheeks.

"I don't know, Vinnie. There must be relatives."

"The poor child," he said. "Not only does she lose her mother, but her father, too."

"Her father killed her mother, Vin," I said, "don't forget that."

"I feel sorry for her."

"Don't worry about her too much," I said, "the little Lisa I know will survive. Besides, all I care about is that you're off the hook."

"I owe you a lot, Nick," he said, touching my arm.

"Just buy me a place in heaven, big brother," I said teasingly.

Sam gave me a look across the table that said, "How could you?" just before my brother said, "Nick, what a thing to say!"

His tone was disapproving.

Things were finally back to normal.

The employees of Thorndike Press hope you have enjoyed this Large Print book. All our Large Print titles are designed for easy reading, and all our books are made to last. Other Thorndike Press Large Print books are available at your library, through selected bookstores, or directly from the publishers.

For more information about titles, please call:

(800) 223-1244

To share your comments, please write:

Publisher
Thorndike Press
295 Kennedy Memorial Drive
Waterville, ME 04901